SUBWAY TOKENS
IN THE SAND

Books by Wendy Lee Nentwig
from Bethany House Publishers

Unmistakably Cooper Ellis

1. *Tripping Over Skyscrapers*
2. *Moonstruck in Manhattan*
3. *Subway Tokens in the Sand*

UNMISTAKABLY 3 COOPER ELLIS

SUBWAY TOKENS IN THE SAND

WENDY LEE NENTWIG

BETHANY HOUSE PUBLISHERS
MINNEAPOLIS, MINNESOTA 55438

Subway Tokens in the Sand
Copyright © 1999
Wendy Lee Nentwig

Cover illustration by William Graf
Cover design by Lookout Design Group

Published by Bethany House Publishers
A Ministry of Bethany Fellowship International
11400 Hampshire Avenue South
Minneapolis, Minnesota 55438
www.bethanyhouse.com

Printed in the United States of America by
Bethany Press International, Minneapolis, Minnesota 55438

Library of Congress Cataloging-in-Publication Data

CIP data applied for

ISBN 0–7642–2067–5   CIP

For Robin Jones Gunn,
not just because you paved the way,
but because you've been there through fourteen long years
with advice, support, and Shaun Cassidy memorabilia.
Thanks for showing me how it's done.

IT WAS STRANGE. Fifteen-year-old Cooper Ellis could definitely hear something, but the voice sounded like it was coming from very far away—as if someone were talking underwater or in slow motion. She tried to focus on the words, on what was being said, but her brain felt as fuzzy as the sounds barely reaching her ears. Then, just as she was about to give up and drift off again, another sound broke through loud and clear.

"Cooper! The least you could do is acknowledge your guest!" Her mother's sharp tone had no trouble penetrating the thick down comforter she was sleeping under, and Cooper reluctantly poked the top of her head out from under her covers, her eyes still closed.

What time is it? Cooper thought. *Am I late for school? Is it even a school day? And what was that about company?* Before she could find any answers, she was verbally accosted again.

"Finally! I've been trying to wake you for the past ten minutes!" Cooper's best friend Claire explained from where she was perched at the foot of the bed.

Rubbing the sleep from her eyes so she could focus, Cooper couldn't help thinking that Claire Hughes hardly qualified as company. They had been friends since practically the time they were born, and their mothers had been friends even longer. The Hugheses' apartment, three floors below her own in the same building on New York City's Upper West Side, was like a second home to Cooper. As a result, Claire had lost her "company" status more than a decade before, at least in Cooper's mind.

"I can't believe you woke me up!" Cooper complained groggily. "And I'm not even late for anything, am I? You call yourself a friend?"

"You had to get up for church anyway, so don't be such a baby. Besides, it's after eight," Claire announced, as if that justified waking her morning-hating friend.

"The clock may say it's after eight, but my body feels like it's the middle of the night. Explain that to me."

"Maybe it has something to do with you getting up so early yesterday for that shoot in Connecticut. Or maybe you were out late last night even though you *said* you were heading right home when you and Josh left. Did you and Josh stay up late talking? Did things get better than they were at the dance? That's what I came up here to find out, you know. I knew I couldn't wait until I saw you at church to hear how your night ended!" Claire exclaimed with uncharacteristic impatience.

It was only then that Cooper remembered last night's dance, her first "real" date with Josh—with anyone, for that matter—and the recent memories started taking shape in her mind. Had he really told her he liked her and wanted to see a lot more of her? Had she just imagined the hansom cab ride through Central Park with a huge moon lighting up the Manhattan sky and Josh's arm around her shoulder? It certainly didn't seem like something that would happen to her. It was too perfect. But her dreams weren't usually even that good, though, so it must have actually happened.

"Hello? Remember me?" Claire asked, waving from the other end of the bed. "Your best friend who sat and listened to Alex whine about you for over an hour at Cuppa Joe last night so you could be alone with Josh? The one who has about ten minutes to hear every detail of your evening before we both have to get ready for church?"

"Oh, um . . . what?" a bewildered Cooper half answered, half asked. She had been so caught up in her own daydream, she forgot her friend was there.

"Your date!" Claire almost shouted, then lowering her voice she repeated, "I want to hear about the rest of your date." The way she was carefully enunciating her words, anyone overhearing would have assumed she were talking to a four-year-old.

"Well, why didn't you just say so?" Cooper teased, a look of innocence on her face.

Claire grabbed the nearest thing she could find, in this case a T-shirt, and threw it at Cooper.

"Okay! Okay!" Cooper said, raising her hands in surrender. "I'll tell you all about it, just stop throwing things. My room's messy enough without your help."

"I won't argue with you there," the always neat and organized Claire said as she surveyed the damage around her. Most of the floor was covered with clothes, books, and magazines, and the desk was piled precariously high with a mound of what appeared to be clean laundry. The closet door was also in its usual open position, its contents spilling out into the room.

Sitting up in bed, but staying firmly tucked beneath her warm covers, Cooper began her story, starting at the point where she and Josh had left Claire and Alex just a few blocks from her apartment building. She told Claire all about the misunderstanding between Josh and herself and how he had never been interested in Reagan—they had just been working together at an after-school job. She also related the details of the hansom cab ride through the park and how wonderful it felt to finally be alone with Josh after an evening of Alex trying to push himself between them.

"That is so cool!" Claire squealed, giving her friend a quick hug. "I'm really, really happy for you."

"I haven't even told you the best part!" Cooper said, extricating herself from the hug. "He didn't just walk me back to the building; he came all the way up to the apartment door and told me that he couldn't imagine wanting to ever date anyone but me, and then he kissed me good-night!"

"AAAHH!" both girls screeched at the same time, causing Cooper's mother to appear in the doorway.

"Are you girls okay or do I need to call 9-1-1?"

"Sorry, Mrs. Ellis," Claire said. "We just got a little excited."

"Yeah, I think we're under control now, though," Cooper added.

"Glad to hear it, girls, but you only have about two more minutes before you both have to start getting ready or church will be over before we even get there," Mrs. Ellis reminded.

"I know," Cooper replied. "We're almost done."

As soon as Cooper's mom headed back down the hallway, Claire leaned in and said, "So you're like an official couple, then, huh?"

Cooper hadn't really thought of it in those terms. She'd never had a real boyfriend and wasn't sure exactly what the criteria was. If Josh said he didn't want to date anyone else, did that mean they were official? Did one kiss mean that? *Maybe I should look up "boyfriend" in the dictionary and see what definition they give*, she thought. Claire obviously didn't share her confusion.

"Well, of course you are!" she announced, answering her own question. "I guess I should get going, though."

Claire was already standing in the doorway when she turned and added, "This is so exciting! Now your whole life is really going to change!"

Change? What exactly did Claire mean? Cooper wondered nervously as she made her way to the bathroom and turned on the shower. She wasn't sure why that ugly six-letter word had the power to strike such fear in her heart, but it did. For as long as she could remember, she had never liked change. New school years, new classrooms, new teachers . . . those were changes Cooper had never had any control over, but she made up for that instability in her personal life. She always hung out with the same friends, ate lunch in the same place, established routines whenever possible. Why hadn't she realized that having a boyfriend had the potential to bring chaos to her carefully ordered world?

The hot water rushing over her as she showered seemed to clear her muddled thoughts, though, and she found herself remembering whom she was talking about. *This is Josh! He's been eating with us for weeks now, and he already hangs out with me and my friends. Things aren't going to be that different. In fact, any changes are sure to be for the better. Now I won't have to spend time wondering how he feels about me. I'll know. That'll be the only noticeable change.*

Satisfied that she had solved that problem, Cooper dressed for church, slipping a heather-gray cotton T-shirt dress over her head and thick-soled white tennis shoes on her feet. After drying her long, dark hair and pulling all but a few wisps up in a clip, she slipped on a little white sweat jacket, grabbed her purse, and headed out into the living room at the same time her mother called out, "Cooper, you're going to make us late!"

"No, I'm not, I'm right here," Cooper said, grinning at her perfect timing.

"But you haven't eaten anything," her mother protested.

At that, Cooper's father produced from behind his back a cinnamon-raisin bagel filled with Cooper's favorite honey-walnut cream cheese.

"You know, one day you're not going to have me to drag you out of bed and your father to get you breakfast. Then what are you going to do?" her mother asked as the elevator carried them to the lobby of their apartment building.

"Oversleep and go hungry, I guess," Cooper joked.

"That's not funny," her mother told her.

"Your mom is right, shorty," her dad said, using his favorite nickname for his five-foot-nine-inch-tall daughter.

"I know," Cooper finally agreed as she climbed into the cab the doorman had hailed for them. "I'm just not a morning person. But I got up on my own yesterday and was even early for that modeling shoot."

"That's right, you were," her mother agreed. "Now, if you could only do that on school days."

"If I promise to work on it, can I eat my bagel in peace?" Cooper asked.

"Of course," her mother said. "We just want you to grow up to be a responsible person. You're not a child anymore, you know. You'll be sixteen in three weeks."

"I'll be happy to remind you that I'm not a child anymore the next time I want to fly out to Seattle on my own to see

Aunt Penny, or take the subway home after dark," Cooper said between bites of bagel.

"If you'd be more responsible about getting up on your own in the morning and being on time, I'm sure we'd be happy to discuss a revision of the rules, wouldn't we, Jack?"

"I think that could be arranged," her dad agreed.

"Fine, I'll start first thing in the morning!" Cooper announced triumphantly. With that decided, she finished her bagel and had just enough time to brush on a little rosy-brown blush and some lip gloss as their cab sped across town. Stowing her makeup back in the little metal army mess kit she had picked up at a secondhand store, Cooper realized that if she was going to be more responsible, she'd have to start by finding ways to actually be ready when she left the house in the morning. That was going to be quite an accomplishment, and she hoped she was up to the task.

❃　　❃　　❃

Entering the college auditorium that served as their church's sanctuary, Cooper suddenly felt nervous. Josh would be here, and she couldn't help feeling a little awkward seeing him after last night. Would he save her a seat? Should she go find him and say hi? What was the protocol? Once again she realized how little she knew about being a couple and was frustrated at the insecurity she felt flowing through her veins. *There really ought to be some sort of manual*, she complained to herself as she followed her parents into a row halfway down the aisle.

"Honey," her mother said, turning toward Cooper, "isn't that Josh over there?" And before Cooper could stop her, she motioned to an area down front and to the right. Then Mrs.

15

Ellis waved as Cooper sank down in her seat, trying to disappear.

"Cooper, dear, I think he's motioning for you to come sit with him. Why don't you go? It's fine with us if you want to join Josh."

Cooper gave her mother a forced smile and worked her way back out of her row to the aisle. *So much for the casual approach*, she thought as she walked toward Josh. She *did* want to sit with him; she just felt ridiculous having her mother involved in making that happen.

"Hey, I wasn't sure if you saw me," Josh said, breaking into Cooper's thoughts. He was smiling at her so warmly that she suddenly became shy. As she took the seat next to him, she felt so adult. Here she was sitting with her *boyfriend* who had *saved her a seat*. Alex had saved her seats before plenty of times, but that was different.

It was funny she was thinking of Alex because at that point she saw him heading their way, Claire in tow. She looked around to see if there were any available seats, but there weren't.

"Maybe we can find four seats together up near the front," Cooper suggested, already reaching down to grab her purse in anticipation of the move.

"It'll be easier for them to find two seats," Josh reasoned. "Besides, the service is about to start."

Cooper felt a little uncomfortable abandoning her friends, especially since neither Josh's nor Alex's parents went to church. As a result, the guys almost always sat together. It was even Alex who had first invited Josh to start coming to church, so she couldn't help feeling a little like she had taken his chair or something.

Before Cooper could give it much thought, though, a forlorn Alex said, "Well, I guess we'll come find you after," before leading Claire farther down the aisle. A few seconds later, Cooper saw the duo moving sideways in that trying-not-to-bump-people's-knees way auditorium seating demanded, and then they disappeared as if swallowed up by the row. She didn't even have time to look back at Josh before the worship band started in.

A few minutes later, during the prayer before the sermon began, Josh reached over while her eyes were closed and took Cooper's hand. It surprised her at first, and she wasn't sure exactly how God felt about holding hands in church, but she had to admit *she* was enjoying it. And it made church seem to go too fast. Josh had dropped her hand after the prayer, but as they stood to sing the final chorus, he put his arm casually around her shoulder, and it was still there when worshipers began clogging the aisles in a mad dash to get out. She and Josh stayed put, but it still took Alex and Claire several minutes to make their way back. When they did, Alex immediately began taking over, which was his usual way.

"If we leave right now, we can make the first showing of that movie I was telling you guys about at lunch the other day," he announced rather than asked.

"But I was hoping to drag Cooper along to that fashion exhibit at the design school, since *you* wouldn't go with me yesterday," Claire countered, shooting Alex a pointed look.

"Claire, it was a *fashion exhibit*," Alex repeated, as if that alone explained everything. "Of course I wouldn't go!"

"We go with you to see all of your weird artsy films we've never heard of," she argued.

"Yes, but everyone loves movies, and you should be grateful I'm exposing you to cinematic masterpieces you would otherwise miss. Fashion exhibits, on the other hand, are not usually a big draw."

"You can be so exasperating. I don't know why I even waste my time arguing with you."

"Because you love me," Alex answered for her, putting his arm around Claire and smiling down at her irresistibly.

If he only knew how true that was, Cooper thought, wincing at Alex's blindly honest assessment and the pain she knew those unreturned feelings were causing Claire.

"So do you girls need to run and tell your parents where we're going?" Alex asked. "Because we really do need to hurry, you know."

"I don't recall any of us agreeing to go to this movie with you," Claire said, picking up their argument again right where they left off.

"No one said it out loud, but it was *implied*," Alex confidently explained. "You're in, aren't you, Josh? You don't want to go to some boring fashion thingie and see a bunch of weird clothes real people wouldn't be caught dead in, do you?"

"Well, actually . . ." Josh said, "I sort of had my own plans for this afternoon. There was somewhere special I wanted to take Cooper."

"Where?" Claire asked before Cooper had a chance to.

"Yeah, I'm sure we'd be willing to consider a change in plans if what you've come up with is better," Alex offered.

"You don't have to change your plans on account of me . . . really," Josh protested.

"I don't mind," Alex said again. "Especially if it will get us out of going where Claire wants. So tell us, what did you have in mind for our little Cooper?"

"That's just it," Josh stammered. "I was sort of planning on taking *just* Cooper."

"Oh," a surprised Alex said before quickly regaining his composure. "Well, we don't always have to do everything together. Claire and I can always go see the movie today, and I guess you guys can catch it later."

"Only if we stop at that exhibit afterward," Claire warned, seeming a bit more forceful now that it was clear Alex's afternoon plans depended on her going along with them.

"Thanks for understanding. Next Sunday we'll do whatever you two want to do, we promise," Josh said. Then he took Cooper's hand and gently pulled her up the aisle, barely allowing her time to wave good-bye to her friends.

Her stomach suddenly began to churn. What had just happened there? How did "she" suddenly become "we" and lose her voice entirely? She was thrilled that Josh wanted to spend the afternoon alone with her, but he could have at least asked. And then he had gone ahead and made plans for them next Sunday, too, without so much as a glance in her direction to see if she minded. Of course, she'd most likely have spent next Sunday with Claire and Alex anyway—she almost always did. She just would have liked to feel as if it were her decision to do so.

Obviously, this whole adjustment to coupledom was going to take a lot more work than she had anticipated.

"SO WHERE ARE WE GOING?" Cooper asked as they exited the college auditorium, her recent frustration quickly giving way to excited curiosity.

"You'll see," Josh answered mysteriously.

"Oh, come on! You have to at least give me a hint," Cooper complained. "It's not fair! Especially since my parents know."

"I *had* to tell them or they wouldn't have let you come!" Josh protested. "I can't expect them to just let me drag their daughter off to some undisclosed location."

"Fine, then, I'll just have to guess based on which direction we head."

"Go right ahead. You'll never figure it out."

They walked on and turned toward the subway station with Cooper paying close attention to which platform they moved toward.

"So . . . we're heading downtown!" she announced as soon as Josh chose a turnstile to go through. It wasn't much of a clue, but she was feeling triumphant at having solved even one small piece of the puzzle.

"That still leaves half the city as a possibility, so you might as well just give up guessing."

"Why don't you just tell me which neighborhood we're going to," she suggested. "Is it SoHo? The East Village? Midtown?"

When Josh just smiled without answering, Cooper didn't give up. "Can't you at least tell me if I'm warm or cold?"

"You're ice cold," Josh said, seeming satisfied that his secret was still safe.

As their train made stop after stop and they continued to stay put, Cooper was running out of ideas about where they might be going. They were below SoHo now and heading toward the tip of Manhattan. All that was left was Chinatown, Tribeca, and Wall Street, and she couldn't imagine anything Josh could have planned for them in any of those three areas.

When they finally emerged from underground and the unpleasant smells of the subway station, Cooper stood face-to-face with Battery Park and, beyond it, the Upper Bay where the Hudson and East Rivers meet. The park was crowded with tourists heading toward Castle Clinton to purchase tickets for the boat ride over to the Statue of Liberty and Ellis Island, and Cooper turned to Josh with a questioning look in her eyes.

"We're not going to the Statue of Liberty, I'll tell you that much," he said in answer to her unspoken question.

"Good. We went for a class trip once, and all I remember is that climbing all those steps inside of her to get to the torch took forever."

"At least you went during the school year! We had to take my cousins when they were visiting last summer. Imagine all those stairs with a bunch of sweaty people crammed inside that statue in the middle of July's billion-degree heat. It was gross."

"Thank you for that wonderful mental image," Cooper replied, laughing at the mind picture he'd painted for her.

"Anytime," he promised, smiling deviously. "I've got a million disgusting stories I could tell you. This city seems to be full of them for some reason."

"It's because there are so many people in such a small space," Cooper surmised.

"Whatever the reason, let's keep going," Josh said, leading Cooper down State Street, which continued to border the park for several blocks.

"I don't mean to alarm you, but it seems we're running out of Manhattan," Cooper pointed out as they neared the edge of what was her whole world.

"I don't think I ever said the surprise was going to be in Manhattan, so that's not really a problem," Josh replied, giving her a larger clue this time.

"Well, New Jersey's that way," she announced as she pointed in the opposite direction of where they were heading, "and my parents don't usually like me going to Brooklyn unless they're with me, so what's left?"

Her sentence was still hanging in the air as they reached the terminal for the Staten Island Ferry.

"Surprise," Josh said unnecessarily. Then, seeming suddenly nervous, he added, "You've never been on it before, have you?"

"No. I always wanted to because it's one of the only untouristy boat rides in the city, but I never had an excuse."

"Well, now you do," he announced. "I wanted to show you where I used to live."

"I completely forgot that you used to live there," Cooper said, remembering the fact now from one of their earliest conversations.

"Yeah, we only moved to Manhattan when I was in

seventh grade so my parents could be closer to the school where they work," Josh explained from his place in line to buy tickets.

"So you're not disappointed?" he asked a moment later, looking away from the attendant who had just taken his small stack of quarters.

"Not at all! I love being out on the water and the idea of exploring somewhere new," Cooper answered, giving his hand a squeeze. All her earlier uneasiness about Josh going ahead and making plans for her without asking had faded away.

"I think I'd like exploring anywhere with you," Josh replied, leaning in close.

Cooper didn't know quite how to respond to the compliment—one more thing she'd have to adjust to—so she was glad when she saw that the bright yellow ferry was ready to take on passengers. But as soon as the boat pulled away, she found out Josh had another surprise in store for her.

"I thought we could have a little picnic," he explained as he began pulling food out of his backpack. "Of course, most of the food's from home, which means it's weird health food stuff, but I was able to grab a few things from the all-night market on the corner by my house this morning to offset that."

Cooper wasn't sure what to expect when he handed her a whole-wheat tortilla with some sort of sprout and bean mixture wrapped up inside. Her earlier bagel had done little to fill her stomach, though, so she was glad to have anything to eat and, after her first tentative bite, was surprised to find the makeshift burrito tasted really good. There was a sauce on it that was delicious, although she couldn't figure out what it was.

"It's lentil salad," Josh explained apologetically.

"It's great," Cooper told him before taking another enthusiastic bite. "What's in it? Do you know?"

"Yes, unfortunately. I'm responsible for dinner two nights a week, but my mom usually supplies me with the recipes ever since I tried sneaking in cheeseburgers one night."

"What's wrong with cheeseburgers?" Cooper asked.

"My parents are vegetarians," Josh answered.

"Ohhh," she replied, nodding her head knowingly.

"Exactly. So now I'm limited to veggie burgers, pasta, tabbouleh, or lentil salad."

"At least you're learning to cook," Cooper offered, impressed at Josh's hidden talent.

"Yeah, but I can only cook things no one but my family would want to eat."

"Your family and me," Cooper added shyly. "Now, tell me what's in this."

"It's just lentils, black beans, corn, and sprouts in this balsamic vinaigrette that's really easy to make. It's supposed to have cilantro in it, but I left that out because I think it's disgusting. It's like eating perfume."

"Hey, I hate it, too! I'm always picking it out of my salsa, which drives my mother crazy. She doesn't understand why I can't just dip my tortilla chips and take what I get," Cooper explained with a laugh.

"We're finding out we have more in common every day!"

"I guess we're just more perfect for each other than we knew," Cooper agreed happily.

After taking a drink from the bottle of water they were sharing, Josh pulled out two packages of peanut butter M&M's and handed one to Cooper. "I remember you telling me these were one of your favorites."

"Thanks, they are," she said, taking the offered candy.

"I also have all-natural fruit rolls, organic apples, and whole-wheat pretzels," Josh said, listing the rest of his provisions. He was busy cleaning up the trash from their "burritos" before the two went out on the deck, where they could feel the cool March breeze off the water.

"Wow, your mom really *is* into eating healthy," Cooper answered, tucking a few errant strands of hair behind her ears so the wind would stop whipping them in her face.

"It hasn't rubbed off on her kids, though, much to her dismay. She used to try to convince me and my older brother that fruit rolls and raisins were candy, but as soon as we were old enough to go to friends' houses to play, we found out the truth. And I still remember when I discovered sugared cereal. That was a wonderful day."

"How old were you?"

"Six. It was my first sleepover, and my friend Caleb pulled out a box of Lucky Charms. I was mesmerized. I ate three bowls."

"You must have been wired if you weren't used to eating all that sugar," Cooper laughed.

"My mom says I was bouncing off the walls when she came to pick me up, but she did start allowing me and my brother, James, to pick out a box of whatever kind of cereal we wanted each year on our birthdays."

"My mom's pretty good about compromising. She tries to get me to eat healthy at meals, but she keeps a lot of junk around to snack on. And she's always trying to feed my friends. If she finds out about your junk food deprivation, she'll be buying Lucky Charms for you to eat whenever you come over."

"That doesn't sound so bad," Josh said.

Before Cooper could comment, they arrived on Staten Island. As soon as they were out of the ferry terminal, though, she picked up where she left off.

"I'm convinced the main reason Alex comes over is to visit my refrigerator, not me," Cooper theorized.

"Does that bother you?" Josh queried.

"What do you mean?"

"I guess I was just wondering if maybe you wished Alex paid more attention to you than your fridge?" Josh asked, carefully rephrasing his question.

"I like having Alex over the same way I like having Claire over. He's my *friend*," Cooper stressed.

"And you've never thought of him in a more . . . romantic way?" Josh continued.

"What are you getting at? Do you think I'm interested in Alex?"

"No. Well, not really. I guess I just can't help feeling like you guys have been so close for so long, and you've only really known me a couple of months."

"Having known Alex since junior high has its drawbacks, you know," Cooper explained. "After all, it means I remember when he thought snapping my bra strap was fun, how he used to wear the same shirt three days in a row without washing it, and when he brought triple-decker butter-and-brown-sugar sandwiches to school for lunch and ate them in exactly three bites, cramming his mouth so full he could barely chew. Trust me, no matter what Alex may have thought at the time, those things did not make him more attractive to me—or any other girl, I think I can safely say."

"Okay, okay. I'm sorry. I guess I just feel like the odd man out sometimes. Like I crashed your private party with Claire and Alex."

"Well, you didn't," Cooper assured him. "There wasn't any party. But even if you had, it would have been a welcome intrusion. Believe me. I do need to warn you, though. I think the reason Alex is being so overprotective lately is that he has some weird idea in his head that he has a crush on me."

"You're just now figuring that out?" Josh asked.

"What do you mean?"

"I mean, I've known he's liked you ever since I started hanging out with you guys."

"How? I didn't know until Claire told me last night, but even then I didn't really believe it."

"Believe it. It's completely obvious."

Cooper didn't know what to say, and as they walked on in silence, she felt as if a wedge had been driven between them. Why did Alex have to decide to suddenly like her after all these years, especially when it had the potential to ruin everything?

WHEN COOPER COULD STAND the silence no more, she decided to change the subject, determined to get their day together back on track.

"So do you miss living on Staten Island?" she asked, looking up at the almost identical boxy houses that lined the street they were on. They were so different from the tall apartment buildings she was used to in Manhattan.

"Sometimes I wish we hadn't left," Josh admitted, seeming as anxious as Cooper to move on from the uncomfortable subject of Alex. "It's so much smaller here, and you know everyone in your neighborhood. Besides, I really liked my old school," he continued. "It was hard making new friends."

"That must have been awful for you," Cooper said sympathetically. "I can't imagine moving. I've lived in the same building and had the same friends forever." As soon as the words were out, she wanted to swallow them back. Would her indirect reference to Alex, even though it included Claire, too, make things weird between them again? When Josh continued without seeming to notice, Cooper let out the breath she hadn't realized she was holding.

"There have also been some good things that have happened as a result of us moving," Josh pointed out. By the smile he gave her, Cooper knew he was talking about her and blushed self-consciously. Everything was back to normal.

"Okay, now, this is the street I grew up on," Josh pointed out after they had walked several more blocks. "And my old elementary school is just down there."

They continued along at a leisurely pace, finally stopping in the schoolyard.

"This was my fourth-grade classroom," Josh explained, motioning to a door with a brass number six stuck on it. As he put his face to the window to peer inside, he continued to explain. "That was my favorite year because I had the best teacher, Miss Riddle. All the younger kids couldn't wait to have her because she used to let us have class outside on the grass. And during science and art she was never worried about the mess we were making with our experiments or projects."

"Maybe we should try to convince her to transfer to Hudson High," Cooper suggested with a smile. "She'd be a welcome change from some of the teachers we have there now."

"I don't think she teaches here anymore," Josh replied with a shrug. "I think I heard something about her getting married and moving to Seattle."

"I have an aunt who lives in Seattle," Cooper exclaimed. "She's my mom's sister, but she's ten years younger and they're complete opposites. Aunt Penny wears almost no makeup, she isn't married, and she works at a group home for teenagers who have no other place to go."

"Well, maybe she and Miss Riddle are friends," Josh ventured. "Wouldn't that be weird?"

"Definitely," Cooper agreed. "I'm trying to convince my parents to let me go stay with Penny this summer, but the last visit didn't go so well."

"You wouldn't be gone for the whole summer, would you?" Josh asked, sounding a little alarmed.

"No way, they'd never agree to that. I'm just hoping to go for a few weeks."

"Good! I'd hate to think that we'd have all that vacation time and not get to spend it together," Josh explained.

Cooper couldn't help being pleasantly surprised. So Josh was counting on them being together during summer break, which was still two months away! She hadn't even dared to let herself think that far ahead and was amazed to find that he had.

They continued walking through the outdoor corridors and peeking inside classroom windows, Josh sharing his memories with Cooper. Finally, after touring everywhere else, they ended up on the playground.

"These monkey bars used to seem so tall!" Josh marveled. "Now I can bump my head on them."

"I probably would have bumped my head on them even back then," Cooper lamented. "I was almost always the tallest person in my class."

"Well, I think you're just the right height now," Josh told her, giving her shoulder an affectionate squeeze.

"It took me a long time to adjust to being this tall. In elementary school I was all arms and legs. And you think I'm clumsy now? I used to walk into walls, furniture, and anything that got in my way. It was horrible. I was one big bruise."

"I'm sure you were just as cute, though, bruises and all," Josh insisted from his new perch on top of the slide.

"I wouldn't be so sure of that," Cooper warned him. She had moved over to the high bars, but it seemed "high" was a relative term in this case. She was dangling from the tallest bar and yet she still had to bend her legs at the knee to not touch the ground. "I think you wouldn't have noticed me at all back then," Cooper continued.

"I guess the important thing is I noticed you now. And I also noticed I'm hungry again. How does ice cream sound?"

"Sure," Cooper said, swinging on the bar one last time.

As Josh took her hand and led her down another street that looked suspiciously like all the others they had already walked, Cooper continued their conversation.

"It's so funny how if your parents hadn't moved to Manhattan or if we hadn't been assigned lab partners or if you hadn't asked about the reading group, we wouldn't be here together," Cooper mused.

"But all of those things did happen, and we are here and that's what's really important," Josh countered.

After sharing a container of gelato, the duo finally headed back to the ferry terminal. It was almost four, and Josh and Cooper had promised her parents she'd be home in time for dinner.

"I don't want to get you back late on only our second date," Josh explained.

Date. The word was still so foreign to Cooper. She couldn't help wondering if it would ever feel familiar, if she would ever stop waiting for someone to pop out of the bushes and tell her it was all a joke. Oh well, if it was a mistake, she was determined to enjoy it for as long as she could.

"Hey, thanks for letting me bore you all afternoon with my childhood memories of life on Staten Island," Josh said a block or so later.

He was loosely holding Cooper's hand when he said it and absently tapping his thumb against the side of her forefinger in time to some beat he heard only in his head. Cooper couldn't help thinking that as long as he kept on doing that, she could listen to him talk about the Pythagorean theorem or the periodic table of elements or even professional wrestling. Of course she didn't say that. She didn't want him to know that he had the power to turn her into a mushy blob of tapioca pudding simply by holding her hand. How embarrassing! She never wanted to be one of *those* girls—all gooey and annoying, living only to have a boyfriend.

"You didn't bore me at all," Cooper finally choked out. "I like knowing stuff about you."

There. That was a reasonable and unemotional answer, she thought, silently congratulating herself on her control.

"Good, because I want you to know everything about me," Josh said enthusiastically, unaware of the conversation Cooper was simultaneously carrying on with herself. "And I want to know everything about you. Your favorite toothpaste, your favorite TV show, your favorite tennis player."

"I don't really like tennis," Cooper admitted, wondering why he thought she would.

"There! Look at how much I'm learning already!"

"There's really not all that much to know. Honest," Cooper told him. She couldn't help being a little afraid that if he continued to quiz her they might find out they didn't have nearly as much in common as they thought, and he might reconsider things. He didn't seem to have any such fears, though.

"I want to know it all anyway," Josh persisted. "I want to know all about you," he finished, giving her hand a squeeze.

Maybe we'll have more in common after all, Cooper told herself, feeling a little of Josh's optimism rub off on her.

On the ferry ride back to Manhattan, sitting on one of the outside benches that ringed the deck, Cooper leaned her head contentedly against Josh's shoulder and closed her eyes. She couldn't believe that only yesterday she had been at a disastrous photo shoot in Connecticut, and last night she had been at the dance feeling miserable because she was sure Josh liked Reagan and not her. Now, less than twenty-four hours later, here she was feeling so close to Josh and completely content with her life.

Maybe she'd been wrong that morning. It looked like being part of a couple was going to be easier than she thought.

"OH MY GOODNESS, JACK! There's a girl at the breakfast
table who looks just like Cooper, but it can't be because I
haven't gone into her room yet to wake her the usual five or
six times," Mrs. Ellis said to her husband while he drank his
morning coffee.

"Ha, ha, very funny," Cooper replied. "It's too early in the
morning for jokes, though. I said I'd work on getting up on
my own, but we never agreed that I'd have a sense of humor
at this obscenely early hour."

"Oh, pardon me. I must have forgotten the no-jokes-
before-ten rule," Mrs. Ellis replied.

"It would appear you did," Cooper teased back. "Now I
think I'm going to go surprise Claire by picking *her* up for
school for a change."

She grabbed her backpack and her *Partridge Family*
lunch box, and after a quick kiss for each of her parents, she
was on her way.

"See you tonight, sweetie," her mom called after her, but
she was already halfway out the door, so she didn't bother
responding.

"Oh my gosh, what's wrong?" Claire said as soon as

Cooper entered her room. "Did something happen yesterday with Josh? Are you okay?"

"I'm fine," Cooper assured her panicked friend. "Why is everyone making such a big deal of me being ready for school a few minutes early?"

"Maybe because you never are?" Claire suggested. "Seriously, I can't remember the last time I didn't have to come upstairs and rush you out the door."

"Well, I'm turning over a new, more responsible leaf starting today."

As they walked the dozen or so blocks to Hudson High, Cooper gave Claire the details of her almost-perfect Sunday with Josh, telling her how he wanted her to know everything about him and to see where he had lived and understand what it meant to him.

"That is s-o-o-o romantic!" Claire gushed. "I spent the afternoon with Alex at that stupid movie that was filmed using some bizarre camera technique that made it hard to watch. I got dizzy just looking at it, and I still felt nauseous all through the fashion exhibit."

"I'm sorry. At least Alex went to the exhibit with you. I hope he wasn't too horrible."

"You know, it's funny. Most days he is so frustrating I have a hard time remembering why I stay friends with him, let alone think about dating him," Claire admitted. "But then he'll do something amazingly sweet like he did at the exhibit."

"What did he do?" Cooper asked, trying not to sound surprised.

"He knew I was feeling sick, but I didn't want to miss anything, so he ran out and got me some aspirin and ginger ale. Then, as we walked through the exhibit, he read all the little cards describing each display to me so my head wouldn't feel any worse. He even made a game out of looking at each outfit and deciding what kind of film it could be a costume for. He had me laughing so hard I almost forgot to pay attention to the clothes."

"That's Alex for you," Cooper agreed. "He can drive you so crazy, but just when you're most annoyed with him he'll really come through for you in a way you didn't expect."

"Yeah, for a guy he's not too bad."

They were still several blocks from the school when Cooper heard someone calling her name. When she turned to look in the direction the voice was coming from, she was pleasantly surprised to find it belonged to Josh.

"I went to your place to pick you up this morning, but your mom said you'd already left," Josh explained between huffs and puffs. He sounded like he'd been running all the way from her apartment building.

"I actually managed to be ready on time this morning," Cooper explained.

"I know you're usually running late, so I thought I had plenty of time to catch you," Josh admitted a little sheepishly.

"Gee, I didn't know my new commitment to being on time was going to have such an immediate effect on everyone around me, and I certainly didn't expect it to be a negative one," Cooper admitted. "First, I almost give Claire a heart attack by showing up in her bedroom this morning, and now you look about ready to drop from having to run after me. It seems my being on time is hazardous to my friends' health!"

"I don't think any of us will suffer any lasting damage," Claire predicted, giving her friend a soothing pat.

"And I found you, so now I'm fine," Josh added.

The trio walked on to school with Josh and Cooper hand-in-hand. And that morning before he caught up to her was one of the only times Cooper was away from Josh all day. He met her at her locker during each break and walked her to every class, even though the gesture likely made him late to his.

"I love seeing so much of you, but it's silly for you to rack up a bunch of tardies just to spend a few minutes with me between classes," Cooper pointed out. "You're going to end up with a detention."

"I was late to one class," Josh said, waving his hand dismissively.

"But if you're late to that same class two more times, it's an hour after school," Cooper reminded.

"I guess we'll just have to walk faster, then, won't we?" Josh said with a smile that melted Cooper's insides. As she smiled back at him, he put his arm around her shoulders and hurried her along to her English class. Once she was safely delivered to the doorway of her classroom, he gave her a quick peck on her cheek before taking off toward the math wing at a sprint.

After biology class, Josh insisted on carrying Cooper's lunch as well as his own, and he was extremely attentive throughout the entire break, which is why Cooper couldn't understand the vaguely uneasy feeling in the pit of her stomach. She chalked it up to nerves and was glad when it calmed down during fifth period. The unidentified feeling returned when Cooper found Josh waiting for her at her locker after school, ready to walk her home. This time she attributed it to the confrontation she knew was scheduled with her modeling agency.

"I'm meeting my mom at Yakomina Models to talk with

my booker, Tara, about some problems with Saturday's shoot," Cooper explained. She knew that even if she wanted to, she couldn't have changed her plans. The funny thing was, as much as she dreaded the meeting, she didn't really want to. She loved being near Josh, but she'd barely had time to think a private thought all day. He was always so close by. She had to admit she was eager for a few minutes to herself, even if they were to be spent on New York City public transportation.

"Oh, I was hoping we could study together. We have that dumb handout from biology to do tonight," a dejected Josh told her. "At least I can walk with you to the subway," he consoled himself.

"Sure," Cooper agreed, heading for the double doors that would lead outside. Before she descended the stairs into the underground station, Josh made her promise to call him as soon as she got home. Maybe there would still be time for a quick study date, he suggested.

Not until Cooper was on the train that would take her to the other train that would take her to the Yakomina offices did she lean her head back against the grimy, thick plastic window of the subway car and shut her eyes. She couldn't figure out why she felt so exhausted. She was glad when she finally arrived at her destination and could put her worries on the back burner, at least for a little while.

❈   ❈   ❈

"I can understand why you're upset," Tara said to Cooper and her mom after they had related the details of Saturday's disastrous shoot. "We do everything in our power to ensure our models don't end up in situations like this, but sometimes things are out of our control."

"So what can we do to prevent this from happening to Cooper again?" Mrs. Ellis asked, cutting through the niceties to the solution.

Sometimes her mother's blunt, straightforward manner embarrassed Cooper, but today she was glad to have her on her side. Cooper knew she couldn't have been nearly as forceful and yet she also knew she didn't want to go through another shoot like last weekend's.

"There are several precautions you can take. First, I'd consider getting Cooper a cellular phone. That gives her the power to call if anything remotely questionable comes up without her even having to leave the shoot. Also, some emergency money tucked away in her bag is always a good idea."

Cooper found herself nodding in unison with her mom. Those sounded like fairly simple solutions, but she found herself a little disappointed. Deep down she had hoped Tara would tell her how to make sure she was never in such an uncomfortable situation again instead of just how to get out of the next one.

"Isn't there any way to avoid men like Roelant Guldner altogether?" Cooper asked, still clinging to that distant hope.

"Don't I wish!" Tara replied. "I try my best to listen to the buzz about people and steer my models clear of anyone I know is dangerous, but in the end it really rests on your shoulders. I know it may not seem fair, but it's your responsibility to speak up when you know a situation isn't right. It is always your choice to walk away from a shoot you don't feel comfortable with. Of course, I'd prefer a phone call first," Tara added, "but no job is worth putting your safety or future at risk."

"So how would I have walked away from Saturday's shoot?" Cooper queried.

"I admit, that would have been a difficult one. You were pretty much stranded out there in Connecticut. I probably shouldn't have sent you on a shoot outside of Manhattan while you were still so inexperienced, but you handled things just as I would have. I'm proud of you."

"Thanks," Cooper replied.

"Now, if you had told me Roelant was bothering you at the earlier shoot, I would have been able to turn down the second job when it came up and you would have been spared this whole mess," Tara reminded Cooper.

"I know, I know," Cooper said. It was something she'd told herself a million times in the past few days. "I'm sorry I didn't tell you right away. I just felt like maybe I was over-reacting."

"He's twice your age and he was asking you out. You weren't overreacting," Mrs. Ellis chimed in.

"As strange as it may seem, there are girls Cooper's age in the industry who are on their own and frequently have dinner with men Roelant's age and stay out partying, which is probably why he thought he could get away with it," Tara went on to explain. "I'm not saying it's right; I'm just warning you, Cooper, that this can be an ugly business, and your values are going to come under attack. You're going to have to get used to standing up to people or you're not going to last as a model."

Cooper found herself wondering if she even wanted to last. Was modeling really worth all this?

"I have every confidence in my daughter's ability to take care of herself," Mrs. Ellis said in her forceful way. "Still, maybe it wouldn't be such a bad idea if I accompanied her on shoots for a while."

"You're welcome to do that," Tara agreed. "Just be careful to not get in the way of the actual job. If you start offering advice about the clothes or hair or lighting, it can cost Cooper future jobs. These people don't like unsolicited opinions when they're trying to work."

"I think I can handle that."

"Good," Tara said. "I hope I've been able to put your minds at ease, at least a little. And I truly am sorry about Saturday. I think if we all work together we can make sure nothing like that happens again."

"Thanks, Tara," Cooper called out after she and her mom had started moving down the hallway.

✳　　✳　　✳

"Now, that wasn't too bad, was it?" her mother said as soon as she and Cooper were in a cab.

"No, not too," Cooper replied. "I'm glad Tara wasn't mad about Saturday. Even though I know I did the right thing, I was still a little afraid she'd be upset."

"If she had been, I think we would have had to reconsider your modeling career."

"Are you serious?" a disbelieving Cooper asked. "You didn't say anything to me about that before we met with Tara."

"I figured we could cross that bridge if and when we came to it. I don't want you doing anything where you don't feel safe, so we'll see how this new arrangement goes," her mother suggested. "Now, let's talk about something more pleasant, like your birthday."

"That works for me!" Cooper said with more enthusiasm than she'd felt all day. She loved birthdays, and she was sure turning sixteen would be magical.

"The McCormicks are letting us use their beach house again during your spring break, so we'll be in the Hamptons for the celebration this year. Is that okay with you? We can always have your party the week before or the week after, or we could come home a day early, I suppose."

"No, celebrating at the beach sounds great," Cooper agreed. She had already begun envisioning the party: the beach lined with tiki lamps and music mixing softly with the sound of the waves. It would be so different from the usual slumber party with Claire.

"You can have Josh and Alex come out for the day," Mrs. Ellis continued.

Claire and her family always spent spring break with the Ellises and would automatically be there. And maybe she could invite that neighbor guy she and Claire had met last year who had been nice enough to show them around. He and Josh would probably get along great.

"And you'll make Grandma's chocolate angel food with whipped cream frosting?" Cooper asked pleadingly. She knew it took almost a dozen eggs and quite a bit of time, but it was her favorite thing in the whole world.

"If you remind me to bring the angel food pan with us," her mother promised. "Now that we have that settled, let's talk about your present."

Cooper had to bite her tongue. She had been planning to broach the subject of getting a dog, but her mother had caught her off guard. She didn't feel like she had her arguments fully prepared yet. Oh well. She might as well just dive right in.

"I was thinking . . ." Cooper began, but before she had three words out, her mother spoke over her.

"I've decided to redo your room!"

"What?" Cooper asked, all thoughts of dogs drifting immediately from her mind.

"It's been needing some sprucing up, and I thought it would make a wonderful birthday gift," her mother explained. "I can get most of the materials for next to nothing through the shop," she continued, referring to Ellis-Hughes Interiors, the business she and Claire's mom had started several years earlier.

It sounded generous. What almost-sixteen-year-old girl wouldn't want a professional interior designer to redo her bedroom for free? But Cooper knew that while she respected her mother's talent as a designer, they had completely opposite tastes. The rest of the Ellis home was crisp and clean, almost stark, with bleached wood floors and the palest pale upholstery. Cooper's room added the only real color to the apartment. Admittedly, not everything matched and some of it was sort of old, but Cooper wasn't ready for a change. Her room was familiar.

"I have to check on a delivery date—I did special order a few yards of fabric—but I think I can have the whole thing done by the time we return from vacation. Won't that be a nice surprise, honey?"

"Um, sure," Cooper said with little feeling. She knew from experience that once her mom got going, there was no stopping her.

Like it or not, new room here I come.

"COOPER, YOU HAVE A MESSAGE on the machine," her mother called out minutes after they had entered the apartment.

Cooper was sitting on her unmade bed looking forlornly around her room. *What is she going to change?* she wondered. Her worn-until-it-was-flannely-soft comforter cover? That was sure to go. And the "women of the Old Testament" flannelgraphs that she had hung up on her wall after she and Claire had taught the four-year-olds Sunday school class last year? Those were definitely on their way out, too. Good-bye Sarah and Ruth and Naomi and Bathsheba.

With a sigh Cooper made her way to the hall phone to replay her message. *Please, God, let it be good news*, she whispered as the machine rewound its tiny tape.

"Hey, Cooper, it's me, Josh. Just wanted to remind you to call me when you get home. Maybe we can still do our bio homework together if it's not too late. Call me, and I can be right over."

Actually, Cooper felt like vegging out in front of the TV all by herself, but she immediately felt guilty for thinking that. It's not that she didn't want to see Josh, but it seemed silly for him to come all the way back uptown when they had spent all day together at school and they would see each other first thing in the morning. Still, Cooper remembered her vow to be more responsible and quickly adjusted her attitude, reminding herself that being grown-up may actually mean biting her tongue while her mom ruins her perfectly good room. It may also mean if she's going to be a girlfriend she has to get used to doing what Josh wants, too. With that in mind, she carried the cordless phone back to her room and dialed Josh's number.

❊　　❊　　❊

"Josh, why don't you stay for dinner?" Mrs. Ellis suggested, appearing in the kitchen seemingly from out of nowhere. "Will your parents mind? I'm making vegetarian lasagna."

Cooper and Josh looked at each other and laughed. "I just can't escape! It's a conspiracy to keep me from eating meat!" Josh whispered.

When she was able to stop laughing and regain her composure, Cooper explained to her mom, "Josh's parents are vegetarians, so he barely ever gets to eat meat. It's just funny that you invite him to eat over and it's a vegetarian meal."

"That is quite a coincidence," Mrs. Ellis agreed.

"But I'd love to stay," Josh interjected. "Vegetarian lasagna is fine with me."

"No, I wouldn't dream of it. You call and clear it with your mom, and I'll thaw out some nice steaks. We can grill those instead as long as your parents don't mind. I'd hate for them to think I'm corrupting you with beef. They may not let you come over anymore."

"Oh, it's fine. I can eat whatever I want when I'm outside

of the house. Mom just refuses to buy any kind of meat and most processed foods herself," Josh explained a little self-consciously. "I'll call and make sure it's okay for me to stay, though," he continued before adding, "It's Dad's night to cook, so I sure hope they give me the green light."

Josh returned to the table a few minutes later, smiling from ear to ear.

"No problem," he announced to both Cooper and Mrs. Ellis.

"Great! As soon as Mr. Ellis gets home, we'll put these steaks on the grill. I'm so glad you can stay, Josh."

"See! I told you she loves to feed people," Cooper whispered.

"That's fine with me," Josh said with great enthusiasm. "Now, let's finish these last two questions so we can forget about homework for at least a little while."

Just as they were gathering up their biology books and clearing the table, Mr. Ellis came through the door. By the time he entered the kitchen he already had his tie hanging loosely around his neck and the top two buttons of his dress shirt undone.

"Hi, shorty," he said to Cooper, messing up her hair in his annoyingly endearing way. While she released her dark brown ponytail so she could smooth everything back into place, her dad looked at Josh blankly.

"Oh, we have company! Where are my manners? Good to see you again, Jim, uh . . . I mean, John."

"It's Josh," Cooper's probably soon-to-be ex-boyfriend mumbled without meeting anyone's eyes.

"Dad, stop it right now. That is *not* funny!" Cooper loudly warned. Turning to Josh, she tried to explain. "He knows your name perfectly well. He's just teasing, but he's *not*

funny." The last few words were more for her father's benefit
than Josh's. Oooh! Why couldn't she have a dad like Claire's,
who traveled a lot and was rarely home to humiliate her?

"I'm sorry," Mr. Ellis said, managing to look truly repen-
tant. But then he added, "It's just hard to keep all of Cooper's
boyfriends straight. I guess John was last night."

"Okay, I'm not kidding!" Cooper practically shouted. "No
one is amused! And you know there is no John." When she
saw a smile playing at the corners of her dad's lips, she knew
she was getting nowhere, so she tried a new tactic and ap-
pealed to her mother. "Can't you make him stop? Please?"
She was pleading now.

"Jack, stop tormenting your daughter or I'll burn your
steak," Mrs. Ellis threatened.

"Okay, you win. I'll go change my clothes. But you really
know how to hit a guy where he's vulnerable—right in the
stomach," he told his wife before heading down the hall to
the master bedroom.

"I'm really, really sorry about that," Cooper said as soon
as she and Josh were in the living room, out of her parents'
earshot. "Try not to take it personally. He does that to everyone. He called Alex 'Allen' for more than a year just to be
annoying. I keep threatening not to bring people home anymore, but I guess he knows I'm bluffing, so he keeps it up."

"Is that what happened? He scared Jim and John away?"
Josh teased.

Cooper reached behind her on the couch, grabbed one
of the off-white pillows, and smacked Josh square in the face
with it. "You know, you're about as funny as my dad!"

"Just for that, I get control of the remote," Josh announced, pushing the TV's power button.

Cooper and Josh were comfortably settled on opposite

ends of the couch watching *Gunsmoke* when her dad returned, having traded his boring navy suit for a pair of khakis and a red polo shirt.

"She can be quite a handful, Josh, so I'll be in the kitchen if you need me," Mr. Ellis said as he passed the pair. "And don't let her force you to watch any of those sappy shows she's always trying to get me to sit through."

"Sappy shows?" Josh queried, his interest obviously piqued. "What sappy shows is he talking about?"

"I have no idea," an indignant Cooper replied. "I don't watch anything sappy."

"Why don't you give me names of some programs and I'll be the judge of that."

"Some judge!" Cooper charged. "You have fifty-four channels to choose from and we're watching *Gunsmoke*."

"Okay, what would you have chosen?"

"Well . . ." Cooper stalled, trying to look thoughtful. "I like all the old stuff on TV Land like *Family Affair* and *Green Acres* and even *My Three Sons*," she admitted.

"*Family Affair* and *Green Acres*? That's what you watch?" Josh seemed surprised.

"Yes!" Cooper replied, undeterred by his skepticism. "They're great. Take *Family Affair*. It's supposed to be set in New York City, but Central Park is only about as big as our apartment, so Buffy and Jody are always playing on the same tiny patch of Astroturf. And you have to love *Green Acres* because it has a pig that watches TV and stays in hotels. How can you pass that up?"

"Easy. Just like this," Josh said, aiming the remote and turning to ESPN.

"Now, this is a waste of a channel," Cooper announced.

"Are you kidding? This is the best thing to happen to

cable TV since, well, cable TV!"

"Oh puh-lease! This is only slightly less boring than C-Span."

"Ouch, that hurt!" Josh countered. "I can't believe you have the nerve to say anything negative about the modern miracle that is ESPN. That's just wrong."

"Ha, ha, ha. You're just lucky dinner is almost ready or I'd be fighting you for that remote. Speaking of which, I'm gonna go see if Mom needs any help. I'll be right back."

"Let me know if she does. I can help, too, you know. I'm very handy with sharp knives."

"I just bet you are," Cooper replied before disappearing into the kitchen. When she reappeared a few seconds later, she announced with a straight face, "Dinner's ready, *Jim*. Come and eat!"

"So that sense of humor runs in the family, huh?" Josh asked as he followed Cooper toward the wonderful smells emanating from the Ellises' kitchen.

"How's that paper on Winston Churchill coming along?" Mr. Ellis asked Josh after leading everyone in a prayer and then loading his plate with a thick slab of beef and generous helpings of roasted potatoes and Caesar salad. "I was serious about my offer to loan you any books you think might be helpful."

Cooper felt her insides melt a little. Her dad, even though he could be so maddening with all his teasing, was genuinely nice and always took an interest in her friends without ever prying. And her mom, as much as she could drive Cooper crazy sometimes, was so sweet making sure Josh had more food than he could possibly eat. Sometimes—usually when she least expected it—her parents could be really great.

The rest of the meal was uneventful, with Cooper's parents behaving amazingly well. As she walked Josh to the door later that evening, he said, "This was way better than some dumb old band practice."

"What?" Cooper asked, genuinely confused.

"I didn't tell you that Bob and some of the guys are starting a band and wanted me to join?" Josh asked.

"No, but that's great!" Cooper enthused. "When are you guys getting started?"

"Oh, well, they started practicing tonight," Josh explained. "But I told them I wasn't interested."

"Why?"

"Because they're rehearsing three nights a week," Josh said, as if that explained everything.

"So? What's wrong with that?"

"I'd barely get to see you!"

"It's only three nights," Cooper pointed out. "You see me every day at school, sometimes after school, and most of the weekend, too."

"But sometimes you're working after school and on Saturdays. I don't want to be off with the band during the only time you're free."

"I think that's really sweet," Cooper admitted, softening a little, "but I still think you should reconsider. We'll always be able to find time to spend together. Besides, it sounds like it would be really cool, and you've been practicing on your guitar a lot lately. The song you played for me over the phone the other day sounded great."

"I'll think about it," Josh finally conceded.

"That's all I ask," she said as he headed for the elevator.

Later that evening, as she buttoned the oversized flannel pajama top she had inherited from her dad's drawer a few months back, Cooper couldn't believe how tired she was.

She'd had a wonderful day with Josh, but being a girlfriend was exhausting! And she hadn't talked to Alex or Claire, which felt really strange. Worse, she hadn't talked to God much, either. Still, with her droopy eyelids she glanced guiltily at her Bible sitting on the edge of her disorganized desk and left it undisturbed. Instead, she turned out the lights and rolled over. Tomorrow she'd get back on track, she promised herself. Tomorrow she'd make it up to God for sure.

WHEN HER ALARM PIERCED HER DREAMS much too early the next morning, Cooper quickly slapped at the Snooze button and burrowed back down under her familiar covers, a habit she'd practiced for as many years as she'd had her own clock by her bed. Just as she was about to ease back into sleep, though, she remembered her promise to herself to be more responsible; and although it took almost every ounce of determination she had, she sat up, rubbed the sleep from her steel gray eyes, and trudged off toward the bathroom. Maybe a steamy shower would help, but Cooper doubted it. No matter how much of an effort she made, she knew she would never be a morning person.

Somehow she managed to dry her hair, apply her makeup without poking herself in the eye or smudging anything that shouldn't be smudged, and get dressed in record time. When she showed up in the kitchen, her mother seemed even more surprised than the day before.

"Two days in a row! I was sure yesterday was just a fluke," Mrs. Ellis said.

"Nope. I'm a whole new me," Cooper announced with as much enthusiasm as she could muster that early in the morning.

"I don't think you need to go that far. I don't want a new daughter, just a slightly more responsible one."

"Order received and processed," Cooper replied before turning her attention to more important things, like rummaging around in the cupboard for some cereal.

Out of habit from years of running late, she wolfed down her cereal and was rushing out the door with her arms loaded down with her lunch, backpack, jacket, and purse when she backed into something unfamiliar.

"Whaaa. . . ?" she blurted out as she turned to face Josh, dropping her lunch box on his right foot, followed by her little metal purse on his left.

"Hey! Ow!" he replied. Cooper waited for him to say more, but he seemed too stunned by the assault to form words with more than one syllable.

"Oh, I'm so sorry!" Cooper finally cried, reaching down to pick up her wayward belongings. "Are you okay? Did I break your toes? Do you want to sit down?"

"No, it's my fault," Josh insisted when he could finally speak. "I guess I scared you, lurking in your hallway."

"Actually, you sort of did," Cooper admitted. "Did you just get here?"

"About ten minutes ago. I didn't want to miss you like yesterday, but then I got here and realized I probably shouldn't ring your doorbell so early in the morning."

"That was very thoughtful of you. My parents are always up before the sun, though. You would have been fine."

"I'll remember that tomorrow and save my feet some grief," Josh said as they walked to the elevator.

"Now, are you sure you're okay? I feel so bad. I practically crippled you!"

"I'm fine, but you know, if you would carry your lunch

in a paper bag like most people it would have hurt a lot less. Where did you get that thing?" Josh asked, pointing to her metal *Partridge Family* lunch box.

"Believe it or not, it was my mom's when she was in elementary school. She had a huge crush on Keith—see, he's the one here with the funkadelic shag haircut. I found it in my grandparents' garage when I was in junior high, and she said I could have it. I've used it ever since. Isn't it great?"

"But that show is so old, and doesn't the whole family wear velvet pantsuits or something?"

"Okay, I admit the clothes are a fashion crime, but the reruns are wonderfully cheesy," Cooper explained before adding, "and *definitely* better than anything on ESPN."

"Wait a minute! Let's not get into that again. Hurry and ring Claire's doorbell before you say something you'll regret."

"I'll stop for now, but the next time you're over, we're watching *The Partridge Family*, not ESPN," Cooper warned.

"*The Partridge Family* isn't even on," Josh said just as Claire opened her front door and, without missing a beat, jumped into the conversation.

"It doesn't have to be on. Cooper has at least half the episodes on tape."

"You're joking, right?" Josh asked hopefully, looking from Claire to Cooper and back again.

"Not at all. They're just waiting for you upstairs anytime you're ready to watch," Cooper said with a too-sweet smile. She was enjoying this.

"Couldn't we just make some sort of agreement that I won't force you to watch ESPN if you won't force me to watch *The Partridge Family*? I'd be really open to that," Josh said.

"Um, guys?" Claire interrupted. "Can we save any pacts or deals for the walk to school, or do they need to be made here in the hallway?" Then, without waiting for an answer, she headed for the elevator, slipping her arms into her jacket as she walked.

"I see no reason to make any deals," Cooper continued once they were outside in the brisk March air. "I mean, I already watched ESPN with you, so it seems only fair that it's my turn to pick a show now."

"Oh man," Josh sighed in resignation. "I'm not going to get out of this, am I?"

"Nope," both girls answered in unison.

"You said you wanted to know all about me—even my favorite TV shows," Cooper reminded.

"Maybe I was wrong. We should have started with something easier, like your favorite kind of gum or something."

"Too late now," Cooper said.

❅   ❅   ❅

"Are you aware of your friend's obsession with really bad, really old TV shows?" Josh asked Alex when he plopped down next to him in the enclosed atrium where the group always ate lunch.

"Which really bad show are you referring to and which friend?" Alex asked. "They both like so many."

"Cooper and her *Partridge Family* fixation," Josh explained. "And as if it isn't bad enough that she likes that stuff, she's actually going to force me to watch it with her."

"No sweat. That show isn't bad at all. I even taped some of those for Cooper. You really have to worry when she starts trying to get you to watch *The Flying Nun*. That's one of her favorites at the Museum of Radio and Television, and it's so bad, words don't even describe it."

"Excuse me? You can stop talking about me like I'm not here," Cooper interjected before rolling her eyes in Claire's direction.

"You don't have any episodes of *The Flying Nun* on tape, do you?" Josh cautiously asked.

"Sadly, no. But maybe someday, if you're lucky, they'll start airing it again."

"That would be a happy day, indeed," Josh agreed, but with all the sincerity of a used-car salesman.

"Now that I've given you fair warning about what's in store for you," Alex said to Josh, "why don't we move on to more important topics, like plans for spring break. It's only a week and a half away."

"What did you have in mind?" Josh asked.

"That depends. Are you girls off to the beach again?"

"Yeah," Claire managed to say between bites of yogurt.

"What beach?" Josh asked, looking to Cooper for details.

"Oh, some client from our moms' interior design business lets us use this house they have on Long Island for a week every year in the spring—they only use it in the summer or something—so that's what we always do over vacation."

"And they leave their poor friend Alex behind in the smelly, crowded city all alone," Alex complained.

"You love this smelly, crowded city, and you know it," Claire reminded him without a touch of sympathy.

"All the same, maybe you could appeal to your respective parents to include me in this year's festivities. You both know my family never goes anywhere," Alex suggested, then in a more desperate tone added, " 'Help me, Obi-Wan Kenobi. You're my only hope!' "

"Nice *Star Wars* reference, Mr. Movies, but I don't know if that's going to fly with the higher-ups," Cooper replied.

"But your parents love me!" Alex insisted. "Both of you girls' parents adore me, and you know it!"

" 'Adore' may be a bit strong," Claire said, eyeing her friend skeptically.

"Maybe you can come out one day on the train," Cooper helpfully suggested.

"One day? One day! Is that all I mean to you?"

"Oh brother!" Cooper said. "I think you should consider acting instead of directing as a future career. That little performance was positively Oscar worthy."

"Thank you very much for noticing. Now, if you'll take me to the beach with you, I promise to thank you in my very first acceptance speech when I'm famous."

"That's an honor I may have to do without."

"Too bad," Josh said, not sounding entirely like he thought it was. Cooper didn't pick up any malice in his tone, but she got the distinct feeling he was glad Alex wouldn't be accompanying her to the beach.

"I guess we guys will be taking the train out, then," Alex told Josh. "At least it will be nice to have someone to ride with."

Cooper hadn't even thought about Josh coming. It was that whole getting-used-to-having-a-boyfriend thing again. It made sense, though. It wasn't a horribly long train ride, and if Alex could visit, Josh could just as easily come, too. She'd have to remember to clear it with her parents sometime soon.

"I'll check with my mom about what day would be best for you guys to come out," Cooper promised.

"Just one day?" Alex whined. "You'll be gone a whole week!"

"You'll be fine," Cooper consoled. "It's good practice for you. Pain and loneliness are great inspirations for artists. If you're going to make good movies one day, you'll need to go through some rough times. Just think of it as our little contribution to your film career. A gift from Claire and me."

When Josh walked her to her locker a few minutes later, he put in his own bid to occupy her time during spring break. "Are you sure you have to go for the whole week?"

"Yeah, pretty sure. Besides, it's always nice to get away. It's so relaxing there, and Claire and I just lie around on the sand all day. I'm looking forward to it."

"Well, then, you *have* to talk to your parents about letting me come visit a lot, okay? Surely I rate more than one day like Alex gets, don't I? I'm your boyfriend, after all, and I don't want to not see you for a whole week."

"I'll see what I can do," Cooper promised for the second time in less than fifteen minutes.

❋　　❋　　❋

The rest of the week flew by like a speeding car on the autobahn. Cooper was barely ever alone. Josh came over after school on Tuesday and complained through two episodes of *The Partridge Family*. Wednesday she went with her mom to get her new cell phone, which she had to pay for with her own money, and then afterward she met Josh, Claire, and Alex at Cuppa Joe. They were supposed to study, but Cooper didn't accomplish much. She and Claire spent another hour studying when they got back to the Ellises' apartment, and then Josh called her before she went to bed. Thursday they had the reading group, and then Josh wanted to go Rollerblading. That night, Cooper had dinner out with her parents, who were complaining they never saw her any-more, and before she knew it, it was Friday.

By now it was expected that Josh would pick her up for school. She enjoyed his company and felt special that he went out of his way to spend time with her, but she barely ever had time to talk to Claire anymore since he walked her to every class and to and from school. She was starting to feel almost suffocated but didn't know what to do to make things any different.

Josh was great, but she had no idea being his girlfriend would mean spending every waking hour with him. And while Claire had been understanding, Cooper knew she was feeling left out. To fix that, at lunch that day Cooper convinced her friend to accompany her on a quick trip to the bathroom so she could vent her frustrations and make some plans.

"What's up?" Claire asked as soon as they were behind the protective metal door of the ladies' room. Cooper wasn't one of those girls who needed company to walk to the bath-room, so Claire knew there was something going on.

Cooper settled herself on the edge of one of the chipped white sinks. When she was as comfortable as she could be, she plunged ahead. "Okay, here's the deal. I feel really bad, but I don't want Alex to come to the beach and I don't even really want Josh to come. Everything's been so crazy, and being in a relationship is so much work that I just want to hang out with you like we used to. Is that horrible?"

"No! Not at all!" Claire told her. "The way things have been with Alex and me lately, I wasn't really eager for him to come, either. But I figured you'd want Josh there, so we might as well have them both."

"It's weird," Cooper explained. "I like Josh a lot and we

have fun together, but now we're together so much that it's not special. Also, when we're together I always feel like I have to be in 'girlfriend mode.' "

"What do you mean, 'girlfriend mode'?"

"I mean it's not like when I'm just with you or even Alex. I have to worry more about what I say, how I look. And then I have to be sure to sit by him and not pay more attention to anyone else. Like at Cuppa Joe the other night. I sat by you so we could both work on our math homework, and while he didn't say anything, I got the feeling he was disappointed. And then Alex only complicates things. It's just too much work and too much to think about every day, all day. On vacation I want to sit around with you and paint our finger-nails and toes different colors and not put any makeup on and wear my favorite ripped-up old T-shirt and not care!"

"That sounds great to me," Claire agreed.

"So what do I tell the guys? I promised I'd ask my parents, and I don't want to be dishonest."

"Maybe your parents will say no, and then we're off the hook," Claire suggested.

"That's a possibility. I'll wait and ask this weekend and then figure out what to do. Or maybe the guys will just for-get."

"I doubt it," Claire predicted. As they headed back out to the courtyard where their lunches and Josh and Alex were waiting, she added, "So what are you doing tomorrow? I was thinking of going to that bead shop down in Greenwich Vil-lage to get some supplies so we can make jewelry at the beach house. Do you already have plans with Josh?"

"Not yet and I'd love to go. I want to get some of those little glass beads you made those earrings out of a few months back. I love those," Cooper said. She was feeling better already. She and Claire were going to spend the day together, and vacation was only a week away. The calm didn't last long, though.

"Finally!" Alex said while the girls were still a good ten yards away. "We thought you weren't ever going to come back. As punishment I had to eat one of your cookies, Cooper. That's what you get for abandoning me."

"We didn't abandon you," Cooper pointed out, "and we're back now."

"Good, because we were just talking about what videos I should rent for tonight. We were thinking a beach theme with some of those really fake surf movies from the fifties and sixties. That will really help us get in the mood since this is our last video night before spring break," Alex said.

"It sure will," Cooper agreed with all the enthusiasm of someone about to have a cavity filled.

"Hey, you didn't give us an update. Did you get a chance to ask your parents yet? What did they say? When do we leave for the beach?" Alex asked without pausing for breath, looking expectantly at Cooper.

So much for the guys forgetting.

COOPER MANAGED TO STALL THE GUYS, but she knew that sooner or later she was going to have to ask her mom if they could come out to the beach, too. And if her mom said yes, it was going to be a really long week. Luckily, she had an interview for a possible modeling job after school that day, which meant a much needed rest from worrying about spring break.

What has my life come to, Cooper asked herself as she hurried through Times Square, *that I need a vacation from thinking about my vacation?*

She continued to maneuver her way through the throngs of people on Broadway, then turned right onto 44th Street, rushing past Virgil's Barbecue, a small all-night grocery, and the Lamb's Theater before crossing the street. She looked again at the address on the scrap of paper she had grabbed when she got Tara's call. According to the street number on it, her meeting was at Café Un Deux Trois, but she knew that couldn't be right. Not that she would mind one of the pseudo-French bistro's delicious omelets at that moment, but there was no time to eat. From her spot on the street, she looked up and only then realized there were several floors of apartments or office buildings above. Then she noticed a side door off to the left of the restaurant. She pushed it open and hurried up a narrow flight of stairs before finding the door she needed.

"Cooper Ellis from Yakomina Models," Cooper announced to the less-than-receptive receptionist before taking a seat in the already crowded waiting room with six other girls who looked almost exactly like her. She always found that a bit odd whenever she went on a go-see. Whether it was a magazine looking for someone to appear within its pages or an advertising agency looking for a girl to help sell its client's cleanser or lotion or shaving cream, they always seemed to have a type in mind and would call the agencies and request only girls who fit that certain description.

Cooper got called when they were looking for someone wholesome and young with long, dark hair, and she was starting to recognize some of the other girls who competed against her for jobs. One of them was named Shelby, which Cooper had learned only because she had heard it called when they were waiting together before. She was always dressed perfectly, her clothes looking deliberately casual, and she looked exactly like what Cooper thought a model should, which was a little intimidating. Then there was another girl who Cooper knew only from her icy blue eyes and the beautiful black suede bag she always carried.

Even though the other girls seemed much more polished and professional and acted very mature and grown-up, they were still considered girl-next-door types by the industry, which meant they didn't even get considered for shoots where they wanted someone sophisticated looking. That was fine by Cooper because those were the jobs where they really tried to make girls look older and the clothes were usually a lot more revealing. Cooper was perfectly happy to look like a teenager for at least as long as she was one.

"Shelby Morrison," said a woman with fiery copper hair and trendy dark-framed glasses after appearing from somewhere down the hall.

Watching the retreating frame of the other model, Cooper suddenly felt sick to her stomach. Just as suddenly, other symptoms appeared, too. Her hands were all clammy, and she could feel little beads of sweat forming on her forehead. *Oh no!* Cooper thought. *What if I have to throw up? I don't even know where the bathroom is!* By now she was dizzy, too.

Finally she grabbed her bag and staggered to the receptionist desk. "Excuse me, but can you tell me where the rest room is?" Cooper almost whispered while trying not to look doubled over by the pain in her abdomen.

"Down the hall, then turn right, then turn left and it's on your right," the girl said without even looking up from the magazine she was reading.

The hallways were much too long, and the wild purple pattern of the carpet didn't help her dizziness at all. Finally, inside the cool, tiled sanctuary of the bathroom, Cooper wet some paper towels and held them to her forehead. Slumped against the pale blue wall with her eyes closed, she began to feel a little better and her stomach calmed down some. That was good because she knew that every minute she spent in the bathroom was a minute when they might be calling her name, and then they would assume she had just left without telling anyone. That would make her seem extremely unprofessional, and she was already concerned after the fiasco the weekend before. Not wanting that to happen, Cooper gave her forehead one last swipe, looked in the mirror so she could smooth her hair down, took a deep breath, and headed back out to the reception area.

She hadn't even made it to the chairs, though, when another wave of nausea hit her. There was no way she was going to make it through any sort of interview. She'd be lucky if she made it home and into bed. Seeing no other way out, Cooper gathered up her things, then stopped quickly to explain to the receptionist that she was sick and had to leave— a message she doubted would get passed on.

After stumbling down the stairs and outside, she gratefully sucked in several deep breaths of what New York City tried to pass off as "fresh" air. Even tinged with the scent of car exhaust, trash waiting to be collected, and steam from the street vendors' carts, though, it was somewhat rejuvenating. Cooper felt well enough at least to make her way back down to Broadway, where she'd have a better chance of catching a cab.

She stood on the corner, clutching her stomach with one arm and raising the other gingerly in the air to signal she needed a ride. Because she still felt so horrible, though, she was more meek than usual when trying to flag down a taxi, and three of the bright yellow cars passed her right by. Determined to get home to her warm bed, Cooper trained her eyes on the oncoming traffic, searching for a cab with its light on top lit, the signal that it was available to take on passengers. As soon as she saw the next one, she stepped off the curb and forcefully held her arm out. This one stopped, and a very relieved Cooper collapsed into the backseat.

"Where to?" the driver mumbled through a thick accent only after he had already driven two blocks.

Cooper had been so happy to finally be on her way home that she forgot she hadn't given the driver her address! She rattled off some numbers, and soon they were speeding uptown, past theaters and delis and bookstores until they reached Columbus Circle and then finally Central Park. One left turn and several dollars later, Cooper was standing in front of her building, never so happy to be home.

She was all ready to climb into bed, but by the time she had dumped her things on the floor in her room, she was feeling miraculously better. Her stomach was back to normal, her hands were dry, and the dizziness was becoming a faint memory. As her head cleared, Cooper suddenly realized she'd better call Tara. That thought made her a little queasy again. How was she going to explain what had happened, especially now that she felt fine? A twenty-four-*minute* flu virus? Who ever heard of such a thing?

Cooper dialed the number and waited for the receptionist to put her through to Tara's office.

"Hey, is your appointment done already?" Tara queried as soon as she came on the line. "Do you have good news?"

"Um, not exactly," Cooper stammered.

"What do you mean? You did go, didn't you?"

"Oh yeah, I went."

"Don't tell me you ran into Roelant Guldner or someone from that Connecticut shoot."

"No," Cooper replied. "It was nothing like that."

"Well, what happened? You're making me nervous."

"Sorry. I didn't mean to worry you. It's just that, well, it's so embarrassing."

"Why, did you blow the interview? Did they ask you some question you couldn't answer?"

"I did blow the interview. But it wasn't anything I said. I got sick."

"During the interview?" Tara asked, her voice rising an octave or two.

"No, thankfully. I was still waiting to be called."

From there Cooper told Tara the whole improbable story.

"And you feel fine now?"

"I felt fine as soon as I got home. As soon as I got out of the cab, really," Cooper admitted sheepishly.

"Maybe it was just something you ate," Tara suggested. "Or maybe there were some sort of fumes in the office building. Did it smell weird, like paint or bug spray or anything?"

"Not that I recall. And if it did, no one else seemed bothered by it. Also, I only had peanut butter and jelly for lunch, pretzels, and some kiwi fruit. I don't think any of that could have made me sick."

"It's a mystery," Tara agreed, then added, "Oh well. It's not the end of the world. Take it easy, and I'll call you Monday and see how you're doing."

"Thanks, Tara. And I'm really sorry. I honestly did feel sick."

"I know you did. There was nothing you could have done. We don't want you throwing up in a meeting, after all," Tara pointed out. "I'm sure something else will come up next week, and you'll ace it."

"I'll try," Cooper promised before hanging up the phone.

❊ ❊ ❊

"Why didn't you call me right away?" Mrs. Ellis asked over dinner that night. "What's the point of having a cell phone for emergencies if you don't use it when there is one?"

"It wasn't an emergency; I was just sick," Cooper explained.

"But if you felt that awful, you shouldn't have been wandering the streets alone."

Oh, Mother, you have such a way of making things seem so much more dramatic than they really are, Cooper thought with a sigh.

"It's not like I was wandering the streets, delirious," Cooper pointed out. "I walked one block, hailed a cab, and came right home. I don't think I was in any danger."

"Well, I don't like these dizzy spells. If you aren't feeling better by Monday, you're going to the doctor. I don't want you treating your health lightly," she admonished.

"But I'm feeling better *today!*" Cooper protested. "I'm sure I'll be fine on Monday, too."

"Okay," her dad chimed in. "But if you have any more dizzy spells or headaches, you really do need to let your mother or me know, even if they go away quickly like they did today."

"I promise."

"I think as a precaution you should stay in bed tonight even though you say you're feeling fine," her mother announced.

"Mom!" Cooper almost whined, "Josh is on his way over, and Alex already rented the movies! You can't just cancel video night."

"But you've been sick!"

"For all of thirty minutes, and I'm fine now. Honest. Besides, it will be almost as restful to sit on the couch and watch movies as it will be to lie in bed and watch TV or read, right?"

"I guess it's okay," Mrs. Ellis finally agreed, although a bit reluctantly. "As long as you promise to take it easy. That means no going out for coffee at Cuppa Joe later. I want you to stay inside where it's warm."

"No problem."

"And we'll just be with the Hugheses at that movie theater

across from Lincoln Center," her dad reminded.

"I'll look it up in the phone book so I can leave the number for you in case you get sick again," her mom said.

"That's not necessary," Cooper replied. "Really! I'm fine, as I've said a thousand times. You and Claire's parents just relax and enjoy the movie."

Before her mother could protest, the doorbell rang and Cooper raced off to answer it. It was Alex and Josh. The former quickly pushed his way past Cooper into the apartment and began making himself at home, while the latter paused to say hi.

"How'd your appointment go?" Josh asked.

"Let's just say, not very good," Cooper replied.

"Why? No one was bothering you, were they?"

"No, I just got sick, that's all," Cooper explained for the third time that day.

"You look fine now. Are you feeling okay?"

"Yes, and please don't bring it up in front of my parents. They're on the verge of staying home from their movie because they're convinced I'm going to pass out at any minute and need immediate medical attention."

"Okay. Consider the subject dropped."

"Good. Now I just have to load the dishwasher, and then I'm ready to go," Cooper said. "Why don't you go keep Alex out of trouble."

By the time Cooper had the kitchen back to its pre-dinner clean, Claire still hadn't arrived. She was just about to call down to her apartment when her parents appeared behind her.

"We're leaving, honey," her mom announced, although the jackets they were wearing would have been announcement enough. "Now, remember, if you feel sick at all, you call us at the theater and tell someone to find us. We'll come right home."

"I'll be fine. Now go already. Oh, and when you get to the Hugheses', will you tell Claire to hurry up?"

"We'll let her know you're waiting," her dad promised. Addressing the boys he said, "You guys keep an eye on Cooper, okay? She was sick earlier."

"Da-ad!"

"Just a little precautionary measure," he explained. "You don't want to let it go and then be sick over spring break, do you?"

"That's right!" Mrs. Ellis said, as if it were a revelation. "Spring break is only a week away! Cooper, did you invite the boys out for your birthday celebration?"

"Um, sort of. We talked about them coming out for a day," she explained, willing the subject to be miraculously dropped. Of course, that would have been too convenient. Her life never worked that way.

"So you'll be out on Saturday, then?" Mrs. Ellis asked the boys.

"Whatever day you want, Mrs. E.," Alex answered.

"We're available whenever," Josh added.

"Don't you boys have any other plans for the break?"

"Actually, no," Alex answered innocently.

"You know you're welcome to come with us to the beach. I know Cooper would love it, and there's plenty of room!"

"Thanks! That would be great!" Alex said, looking triumphantly at Cooper.

"Both of you have your parents call me, and I'll fill them in on all the particulars. Tell them you'll be supervised at all times, and we'd be happy to have you. It will make Cooper's birthday that much more special."

That much more special for whom? Cooper couldn't help but wonder.

"**WHAT DO YOU MEAN** they're coming for the whole week?" Claire practically hissed at Cooper as the girls monitored the progress of the microwave popcorn in the kitchen.

"I had nothing to do with it. My mother invited them," Cooper tried to explain.

"Oh great! I hope your mother also plans on coming up with ways to keep Alex busy all week."

"I think she already has," Cooper replied. "Us."

"This is going to be one interesting spring break," Claire predicted.

"Well, if you had been here on time, maybe you could have helped me stop this from happening. Where were you?"

"I was on the phone," Claire answered somewhat vaguely, her cheeks turning pink as she did so.

"Who were you talking to that was so important you couldn't tear yourself away for video night?"

"You remember Matt who we had P.E. with last year?"

"The one who always used to pick you for his volleyball team when he was captain?" Cooper asked.

"He picked *both* of us," Claire corrected.

"No, he picked you, and then you'd always convince him to pick me," Cooper counter-corrected.

"Whatever. That's who I was on the phone with."

"Sooo," Cooper teased. "Matt from freshman P.E., huh?"

"Actually, this semester he's Matt from sophomore English," Claire pointed out.

"Isn't that the class you have with Alex?"

"Yes, and it's been really weird," Claire admitted.

"I should say so!"

"No, really. It's been horrible. Here I've liked Alex for months and—"

"For months?" Cooper interrupted. "You never told me this has been going on for months!"

"Well, it has . . . I mean it had, but that's not the point," Claire said, a hint of exasperation in her voice. "What I'm getting at is I'm ready to move on. It would just be too weird dating Alex—you were right. Besides, he's not interested anyway. So Matt's been sitting by me in English, and after school today he asked for my phone number."

"That is so great! I'm really excited for you, Claire!" Cooper said, giving her best friend a spontaneous hug.

"Thanks. I was really surprised when he caught up with me near my locker, and then again when he called me so soon. He hadn't even had my number for four hours!"

"I'm glad someone's finally beginning to notice how wonderful you are."

"Where's the popcorn?" Alex asked as he burst into the kitchen so suddenly he startled the girls.

"A little jumpy tonight, aren't we, ladies?" Alex said. "And who's noticing how wonderful who is?"

"What?" Claire stalled.

"No one," Cooper added, then handed her nosy friend a freshly popped bag of popcorn and a can of Coke, hoping that would distract him. Of course, it didn't. At least, not enough. Normally they shared everything with Alex, but their recent, weird love triangle threw everything off balance. Now with Claire moving on and Alex seeming to accept Cooper and Josh as a couple, she felt no need to rock the boat.

"You were talking about me, weren't you?" Alex continued as he headed into the living room. "You were saying how you're both finally beginning to realize how wonderful I am and how much you take me for granted, right?"

"You caught us," Cooper admitted.

"Guilty as charged," Claire chimed in. "Now, let's start the first movie."

Mercifully, as soon as the video began to play, Alex made no more noise except for a quiet crunching sound, and that was due more to the popcorn than him, so he couldn't really be held responsible.

They were watching *Beach Blanket Bingo* to get them in the mood for spring break. Cooper had to admit she was enjoying making fun of how the main characters, Frankie and Annette, kept bursting into song, but it was going to take more than that to convince her that having Josh and Alex along on spring break was a good idea.

"Look at how Annette's teased hair stays perfectly styled even after she's been out surfing," Alex pointed out. "Isn't that great? You could never get away with that in movies today."

"I guess if you use enough hair spray anything's possible," Claire said.

"Can I get you anything?" Josh leaned in and asked Cooper before getting up to retrieve another root beer for himself.

"No, thanks, I'm fine."

Another wave of guilt washed over Cooper. She felt like

such a traitor. It wasn't that she didn't like Josh anymore; she definitely did. And when he squeezed her hand gently like he just did before heading off to the kitchen, it still made her feel really special and happy. But she had been looking forward to a break. Now she would have to worry about Alex trying to come between her and Josh and about Josh wanting to spend every minute with her and about Claire feeling left out—and she had a horrible feeling it was going to be a big mess. There was nothing she could do about it now, though. The damage was done. She might as well sit back and watch the movie.

As the final credits rolled, Alex disappeared into the kitchen to forage for more food, and within seconds was yelling, "Cooper, can I have some Oreos?"

"Yes," she yelled from her perch at one end of the couch. "Help yourself."

Then just as Josh began to say something to her, Alex interrupted again.

"Cooper, can I have some ice cream?"

"Yes," she answered, a warning tone in her voice. He knew that any snack food in the Ellis kitchen was fair game for him; he was just doing that to be annoying.

After a few seconds passed without any further requests from the kitchen, Cooper asked Josh what he had been about to say.

"Oh, I was just thinking. It sure is a good thing I decided not to join that band because then I couldn't go to the Hamptons with you over spring break," Josh pointed out.

"Yeah, it's a good thing," Cooper agreed, but there wasn't much feeling behind her words.

When Claire returned from the rest room, Alex started movie number two, *Gidget*, starring Sandra Dee, and Cooper was able to once again focus on the TV screen instead of her friends.

Most of the movie centered around Gidget going to great lengths to get the attention of a guy. She learned to surf, spending all her money on a surfboard, and even bribed her crush to take her to a beach party. When she finally got the guy at the end of the movie, Cooper couldn't help but wish the director had thought to show Gidget and her new boyfriend a month or even a week later. She sure would like to see if, after that wonderful first real date, Gidget still felt it was all worth it.

It sure would be comforting to find out Gidget had a hard time adjusting to coupledom, too, Cooper thought. *She probably didn't, though. They probably lived happily ever after and spent every waking moment together and Sandra Dee loved being a "we" instead of a "me."* Cooper was sure she was just some freak of nature: the only almost-sixteen-year-old girl in the whole world incapable of enjoying having a boyfriend.

❊　　❊　　❊

"So what do you want to do tomorrow?" Josh asked Cooper as they all said their good-byes at her apartment door.

"Oh, I'm going bead shopping with Claire," she said, feeling guilty for the millionth time that week. She should have known that it was expected they would spend their first Saturday as an official couple together.

Josh was obviously disappointed but not easily deterred. "That can't take very long, maybe an hour, right? So what are you doing afterward?" he persisted.

"I haven't thought that far ahead," Cooper admitted.

"If you call me as soon as you get home, we can spend the rest of the day together."

Claire looked at Cooper expectantly. While it was true the girls had only planned to go to the bead shop, it was sort of implied that they would spend the afternoon together since they hadn't spent much time just the two of them lately. It was awkward to explain that to Josh, though, especially in front of Alex, but she knew she had to. She took a deep breath and plunged right in.

"Actually, Claire and I haven't seen much of each other lately, and we'll probably spend most of the afternoon together. I'll call after that, though," Cooper promised, hoping that would appease Josh.

"Oh. Well, I'll miss you, but I understand," Josh replied, much to Cooper's relief.

With that settled, Cooper's company loaded into the elevator that would take Claire three floors down to her own apartment and the boys to street level so they could catch the subway to their respective homes.

Cooper was just snuggling under her covers when she heard her parents come in.

"Any relapses?" her mother asked from the doorway.

It took Cooper a few seconds to realize what she was talking about. She had so many other things on her mind as she got ready to drift off that night that she totally forgot she had been sick earlier.

"Cooper, honey, are you all right?" her dad added when her response wasn't immediately forthcoming.

"I'm fine," Cooper finally said, putting their minds at ease. "Not a twinge, not a pain."

"We're glad to hear it," her parents said in unison, a trick they were able to perform with unsettling regularity, despite being so completely different from each other.

"Thanks."

"Good night, sweetie," her mother called from down the hall just as Cooper turned out her light.

"Sweet dreams," her father added.

Not much chance of that, Cooper thought, sighing into her pillow.

SATURDAY WENT A LONG WAY toward restoring Cooper's faith in her friends and herself. She and Claire had a great time that afternoon, shopping and playing around just like they used to, with very little talk of boys. Later that night, she and Josh went out. He took her to a used record shop where they had old-fashioned listening booths, and they spent the evening huddled together experiencing record after record. The store was only a few blocks from her home, but she had never noticed it before because it was on a side street she'd never had a reason to explore. Afterward, they went to Serendipity on the Upper East Side for gooey ice cream sundaes, and then she was home early because her parents were still convinced she wasn't completely well.

Sunday was a different story altogether, though. Cooper, still working on proving herself more responsible, was dressed, fed, and ready to walk out the door even before her parents that morning, but everything went downhill from there. Claire caught up with the Ellises just as they entered the auditorium/sanctuary, and the two girls took seats down near the front, saving room for Alex and Josh on either side of them. Then the boys came in just as the service was starting, and Alex hurried in to the row, squeezing past the girls to sit on the other side of Claire. By the time he got there, though, someone else had plopped into the seat, leaving Alex nowhere to go but backward and right next to Cooper. Josh was forced to take the seat on the aisle, and it was obvious he wasn't pleased with the seating arrangement. But this time Cooper couldn't blame Alex, and anyway, this was church! Of course she'd like to sit by her boyfriend, but they had sat together the whole night before and she was really tired of playing this stressful game of musical chairs.

Then there were the after-church plans.

"Hey, how about we go hang out in the park?" Josh suggested. "We could play Frisbee or Rollerblade."

"Oh no you don't," Alex said. "Last weekend you promised that you and Cooper would do whatever I wanted this weekend since you bailed on us last Sunday."

"I think that was whatever *we* wanted, O Maker of the Plans," Claire corrected.

"Yeah, right, whatever," Alex absently agreed.

"So what did you have in mind for us?" Cooper asked.

"There's a movie shooting down in the East Village, and I heard they might even be looking for extras for this one crowd scene. I thought we could go hang out down there and watch," Alex explained, his voice filling with excitement.

"And are you sure that's what *we* want to do with our afternoon?" Claire asked pointedly.

"Don't tell me you're not with me on this one?" Alex questioned as if it just now occurred to him that Claire might veto his idea. "After I went to the fashion exhibit with you last weekend without a complaint?"

"You may not have complained once we arrived, but you complained all the way there," Claire reminded. "And besides, you owed me big after taking me to that movie that made me sick!"

"I apologized for that already! How was I supposed to know you could get motion sickness sitting still?"

"I know. I really did appreciate you going with me to the exhibit, so I guess the movie shoot sounds fine with me. There's a store I wanted to check out down there anyway."

"Okay, but only one store," Alex bargained. "You have to promise you won't turn it into a shopping trip."

"Cross my heart," Claire told him.

"So how about it, guys?" Alex asked, looking from Josh to Cooper to Josh again.

Cooper was just about to say, "That sounds fine with me," when Josh spoke first.

"I don't know if I'm really up for that."

"But you promised!" Alex charged.

"I know, but what does it matter if we all go or just you and Claire go? It doesn't sound very fun just standing around all day."

"But you promised!" Alex repeated.

In Cooper's other ear, though, Josh was suggesting, "Couldn't we just go to the park for a little while and meet up with them later?"

Cooper felt torn. She wasn't thrilled about standing around on some seedy East Village sidewalk all day, but Josh was the one who promised, so why was he making *her* choose between him keeping his word or getting his way? Why was no one ever concerned with what she wanted to do?

In the end, after studying everyone's pitifully pleading faces, Cooper announced she would go with Alex and Claire—it seemed only fair. Unfortunately, Josh didn't see it that way. The park wasn't going to be much fun by himself, though, so he tagged along. But he made it clear to Cooper and the others that he wasn't going to have a good time.

It took them over an hour to find the location where the film was being shot, and when they finally did there were so many trucks and police barricades and people surrounding it, they couldn't really see anything. That didn't deter Alex, though. He was happy to just stand around and take in the bustling movie set.

Tons of movies were filmed in New York every year, and Cooper, Claire, and Alex occasionally stumbled upon a set. But they were usually filming inside a building, so all you could see from the street was the scaffolding set up out in front for the lighting technicians, the cameramen, and the white catering trucks. It was more rare to find a larger film company shooting something really big outside. Those were the ones that had the power to tie up traffic for blocks and bring portions of the city to a standstill, and they were so expensive that only big movie companies could afford to do it.

Today's shoot was moderately large, but Alex had no idea who was in the film. He thought it was some big action movie. For an action film, though, there sure was a lot of standing around. Just when Cooper was getting tired of nothing happening, there was some movement in front of her, and the crowd parted a little. Before she knew it, Claire was pulling on her sleeve and dragging her forward. Cooper barely had time to reach out for Josh's hand, adding him to the human chain that Alex was heading.

After fighting their way through the crowd and Cooper almost losing Claire twice, they found themselves with an almost front-row view. Of course, with the police barricades up, they were still a basketball court's length away from the action. Still, they could see people with clipboards scurrying around and dozens of thick cables and wires crisscrossing the ground. They could also see the camera, but there was no cameraman behind it yet. Then there were also a few people sitting off to the side in folding chairs—not director's chairs like they always showed on TV—who Cooper assumed were actors because they were fashionably dressed and their hair looked styled.

"Look! I think they're going to get started," Alex said, pointing to someone with a megaphone who was trying to bring about order.

The man began giving instructions to the crew and to the people lined up along the street.

"We're about to get started," the man in jeans, sneakers, and a flannel shirt announced, "which means we need everyone on the street as quiet as possible. If there's too much noise, we'll have to have the police clear the block," he threatened.

At that, the crowd seemed to settle down quite a bit. Then, about ten minutes later, a cameraman appeared and took his place, and suddenly a scene was being shot. It entailed a man and a woman walking down the street, stopping to talk to another man, whom they argue with, and then hurrying into a nearby apartment building. That was it. But they did it again and again and again. Then they shot the man and woman, standing out on the steps in front of the building and talking. At least, Cooper assumed they were talking; she couldn't actually hear anything from where she stood. That scene had to be redone eight times, and by then Cooper was getting a little bored with moviemaking.

"Alex, can we go soon?" she asked her friend.

"I just want to wait and see if they need any extras," he replied.

Cooper sighed. That would take forever to organize, and her stomach was rumbling.

"We could be in the park right now relaxing under a tree and eating hot dogs," Josh whispered to Cooper.

She simply smiled impartially. She didn't want to get into taking sides between Alex and Josh; she felt stuck in the middle enough already.

It took another thirty minutes of standing around before the man with the megaphone announced they weren't going to be shooting any other scenes that day. The crowd let out a wail of disappointment. Cooper felt bad for Alex, but she was excited about the prospect of getting something to eat. There wasn't a lot to choose from where they were on Second Avenue, but after walking three blocks, Cooper spotted Ess-a-Bagel.

"I knew there were two of them, but I never knew where the other one was!" she said excitedly. The shop's bagels were her favorite, but she always did her bagel buying at their Third Avenue shop in midtown. This one was much smaller. Without even waiting for her friends to agree to eat there, Cooper went inside.

"Can I get a cinnamon raisin bagel with raisin walnut cream cheese, please," Cooper announced more than asked. Only when it was being prepared did she turn to make sure her friends were indeed behind her in line.

"If you guys don't want bagels, we can stop somewhere else, too," Cooper offered. "I just don't know what else is around here and I'm *starving*."

"Bagels are fine," Alex said agreeably, while Claire just shrugged and nodded her head. Only Josh seemed unsure.

"I know it's not a smart thing for a New Yorker to admit, but I'm not a big bagel fan," Josh confessed to Cooper once he joined her in line.

"You're not serious?" a stunned Cooper replied. "Everyone in New York likes bagels! I think there may even be some sort of city ordinance that says you have to eat so many per week or they make you move to New Jersey," she joked.

"I must have missed that on the news," Josh replied.

"That's okay, we can find you something else to eat in just a minute," Cooper promised. "I wasn't planning on eating my bagel here anyway."

Josh seemed appeased by that, but she could tell something else was wrong. He wasn't pouting; it just seemed like he was a little quieter than usual.

Just one more instance when an instruction manual on how to understand guys would be helpful, Cooper thought as she chewed the first delicious bite of her lunch. All she'd had for breakfast was some yogurt with granola stirred in, and that hadn't satisfied her for long.

Claire and Alex were also munching happily as the group headed uptown.

"Now, that store I wanted to go to is supposed to be just a few blocks up," Claire said, studying the street signs to figure out exactly where they were.

"I thought it was closer to First Avenue," Cooper chimed in.

"I guess we'll just have to walk the whole block to find it," Claire replied.

And they ended up doing just that. In fact, they walked all the way around *two* full blocks before finding the secondhand store Claire was searching for. Cooper was just about to follow her friend inside when she turned to Josh and said,

"Oh no! I forgot you still haven't had anything to eat!"

"Everyone was so wrapped up in finding this place, I didn't want to slow down the search," Josh explained.

"Still, you should have spoken up. It's survival of the fittest with this group, and if you don't speak up you'll starve. Do you want to go get something now? There's a pizza place across the street that doesn't look too bad," Cooper suggested.

"Yeah, I could go for a slice or two. I guess I can just meet you guys back here after."

"Don't be silly! I'll come with you so you don't have to eat by yourself."

"Really? You will?"

It sort of irked Cooper that Josh sounded so surprised. Of course she wouldn't just leave him to eat lunch by himself. Things had been so much easier before they were dating, when Josh didn't seem so much like her responsibility. Now she felt like she was constantly running interference, trying to keep everyone happy and losing herself in the process. She didn't know how to explain any of that to Josh, though, and she didn't think she had the nerve even if she could find the right words. Instead, she just said, "Of course. Let me run in and tell Claire and Alex so they don't think we deserted them for good."

"Why didn't he get a bagel?" Alex asked, giving Cooper an odd look.

"Because he doesn't like bagels," she explained, hoping that would be enough information to satisfy Alex but knowing instinctively that it wouldn't.

"How can anyone not like bagels?"

"I don't know. I guess you'd have to ask Josh," she told her friend.

It never ends! Cooper thought. *Now I'm defending his taste in food. Why is everyone asking me everything? Just because I'm dating Josh doesn't mean I'm the authority on everything about him. I can't even figure him out most of the time myself,* she wanted to scream. Instead, she just said, "We'll see you guys in a few minutes," and went back out front to where Josh was waiting for her.

"Two slices of pepperoni and mushroom," Josh ordered.

"Mushrooms?" Cooper repeated, wrinkling her nose as she said the word.

"Yes, mushrooms. What's wrong with that?" Josh asked.

"Nothing, it's just that, well, they're a fungus!" she finally spit out. "They're gross!"

"I guess you won't be wanting a bite of my pizza, then, huh?" Josh asked.

"I think I'll pass, but thanks."

After Josh's offending slices were warmed and he had paid for them, Cooper followed him to a wobbly table looking out onto the street. Then, as she stared at the pizza Josh was quickly devouring, she was reminded of how different today was from last Sunday in Staten Island when they were so in sync and seemed to have everything in common.

"Penny for your thoughts," Josh said between bites.

"I think it'll cost you a little more than that," Cooper joked, knowing she didn't want to share that particular thought with Josh for any amount of money and that if he knew what it was, he wouldn't want to hear it, either. Thankfully, he didn't pursue the subject any further, and in a matter of minutes both pieces of pizza were only a memory.

"Thanks for going with me," Josh said, taking Cooper's hand as they crossed the street.

"My pleasure," Cooper replied.

Inside the wild secondhand shop, the walls were painted in bold red-and-pink stripes, and there were racks of clothing, old toys, records, books, jewelry, wigs, and just about anything imaginable. The collection looked like what you might find in the attic of someone who had really bad taste and a lot of money.

Cooper was examining some shiny white go-go boots and a fringe-trimmed vest on a mannequin when Claire came running up to her.

"Look at this, Cooper! It's a photo biography of Shaun Cassidy!" Claire said, holding out a large, old book with a picture of the '70s teen idol on the cover.

"How bizarre! I haven't thought of him in ages!" Cooper said.

"Remember how we used to watch those Hardy Boys reruns when we were little?" Claire reminisced. One of us would sleep at the other's apartment, and whichever mom was in charge of us for the night would make us get into our pajamas and we'd drag our sleeping bags out in front of the TV."

"They were such nice boys," Cooper said, sighing nostalgically.

"And you were so disappointed when you went to check the Hardy Boys books out at the library and it wasn't Shaun Cassidy and Parker Stevenson on the cover. You refused to read the series at all after that."

"It was a matter of principle."

"So do you want the book?" Claire asked. "I could get it for you for your birthday."

"Are you serious? That would be great!" Cooper said enthusiastically, grabbing for the book so she could page through its contents.

"Ah, ah, ah, ah, ah!" Claire warned. "Not so fast. You'll have to wait until your birthday."

"Oh, come on," Cooper begged. "Just a little peek? My birthday is still two weeks away. I don't know if I can wait that long."

"Well, you'll have to," Claire told her friend unsympathetically.

Cooper was about to begin begging more loudly, knowing that if she even threatened to embarrass Claire, she would give in and let Cooper have a peek at the book. Just as she was ready to begin her performance, though, Josh appeared at her side.

"Are you girls finding anything you can't live without?" he asked.

"No," Cooper answered a little too quickly.

"Why, yes, we are," Claire corrected, her voice way too sweet. "Don't you remember the book?"

"Yes, I remember the book," Cooper told her traitorous friend through clenched teeth.

"Cooper begged me to get this for her for her birthday," Claire explained, holding the book out to Josh. Then, as if that wasn't bad enough, she added, "Were you aware of her huge crush on Shaun Cassidy? He was her first love, you know."

"Thank you for the update, Claire," Cooper said in a way that showed she meant exactly the opposite. "I think that's enough information for Josh to take in for one day."

Once the book was purchased and Cooper was thoroughly embarrassed, the group headed for the subway.

"Whose parents would most appreciate the honor of our presence for the rest of the afternoon?" Alex asked after they had boarded a northbound train.

Cooper and Claire looked at each other and shrugged noncommittally.

"I haven't seen much of your parents lately, Claire," Alex said. "I bet they're missing me terribly. Why don't we go there?"

"I'm sure they'll appreciate you thinking of them," Claire responded.

Alex seemed to know from past experience that that was as close to a yes as he was going to get.

The girls were busy laughing over the thought of Alex being away long enough for either of their parents to miss him, when they reached the 23rd Street subway station and Josh suddenly stood up.

"You're kind of jumping the gun a little," Alex quipped. "We have about five more stops before we're getting off."

"I think I'm going to get off here" was all Josh said in response.

"But why?" Cooper asked. "Can't you come to Claire's for a little while?"

"I'm kind of tired, and I still have some homework to do. I should probably go home."

"Well, if you're sure," Cooper said, giving Josh's hand a squeeze and smiling at him uncertainly as he stepped off the train and onto the platform without even looking back.

She wracked her brain the rest of the way home to figure out what she might have done to upset Josh and make him leave, but Cooper couldn't come up with a single thing. That didn't stop her, though, from being certain his sudden departure was somehow her fault.

"READY FOR SCHOOL?" Josh asked when he arrived at Cooper's front door the next morning.

As they took the elevator down to Claire's apartment, Cooper studied his behavior for any signs he might still be upset. But he seemed so normal and in such a good mood that she started to wonder if maybe she had been imagining things before.

By midweek, though, Cooper was beginning to wish Josh wasn't quite so happy with her. He was with her every minute between classes, before school, after school if she didn't have any appointments, and then evenings when her parents would let her go out. They hung out at Cuppa Joe on Monday night, and he came over and studied with her on Tuesday. When she called before leaving school on Wednesday and found out she had a go-see scheduled in an hour, Cooper had to admit to herself that she felt relieved. It wasn't even the amount of time Josh was spending with her, but the way she felt that no matter how much time she gave him it was never enough. It was strange. He had never been like that before they started dating.

"Well, well, well! What have we here?" Alex demanded

to know, approaching Cooper just as she was stashing her cell phone back in her bag.

"What?" Cooper asked as she spun around to face him. Alex was always giving her a hard time about something, so she could never be sure what he would find to tease her about next.

"What were you just slipping into your bag? Could it be a high-tech piece of electronic equipment, the kind you aren't allowed to have at school?"

"It's just a cell phone, and the rule is you can't use them on school property *during* school hours," Cooper pointed out. "Now, if you'll take note of all the happy students exiting the premises, you'll be able to ascertain that it indeed is now *after* school hours."

"That still doesn't explain why you have a fun new toy and you didn't bother to share that news with your best friend in the whole wide world," Alex persisted melodramatically.

"Yes, I did," Cooper corrected. "Claire knows all about it."

Claire, who was standing on the other side of her, was very amused by that, and Cooper thought she saw Josh suppressing a smile, too. Alex wasn't deterred, though.

"Ouch! That hurt!" Alex cried, pretending to stagger under the verbal blow. "I think I'm bleeding, that remark cut me so deeply!"

"You're a quick healer. I'm sure you'll be fine," Cooper assured him. Then, as a peace offering, she held out the phone for Alex to look over.

"Hey, is this your phone number here that shows up when I turn it on?" he asked after pushing several buttons.

"Yeah. I can program other numbers in, too, but so far I

only have the Yakomina offices, my house, both of my parents' work numbers, and a cab company."

Alex wasn't really listening, though. He was too busy copying down her cell phone number.

"Now we can call you and make it ring during class!" Alex said. He had made copies of the number for Claire and Josh, too. "Or did she already give you guys her number?" he asked suspiciously. "I'm always the last to know!"

"I haven't given the number to anyone but Tara and my parents. The phone's for work and for emergencies, so don't you dare call me and make it ring during class, Alex Morrow, or I'll strangle you!"

"Testy, testy!"

"Why do I even bother reasoning with you?" Cooper asked as she snatched the phone back, making sure it was on in case Tara called her, and put it in the pocket inside her bag.

The foursome walked toward the subway station, with Claire turning off toward home when they got to her and Cooper's street. A few minutes later, on the platform, Alex was still shaking his head and saying, "I can't believe you don't have your best friend's phone number programmed in. I thought we were so close, but I guess I was only fooling myself. I mean nothing to you."

"You can go whine about it all you want. I'm not putting your number in when I can call you perfectly well from home. You're just being ridiculous," Cooper told him. She had to raise her voice toward the end of her little speech when the subway train came rumbling through the station. "Now, come on and get on board before you make me late to my appointment," Cooper urged, tugging at Alex's sleeve.

Once they were seated on the train, she turned her

attention to Josh. "So what are your plans for the afternoon?" she asked.

"I don't know. What time do you think you'll be done?" Josh replied.

"I'm not sure. Go-sees are usually quick. I should be home in a little over an hour," Cooper predicted.

"If you want I can come over and we can work on our lab write-up," Josh offered.

"That sounds fine. I'll call you when I get home."

"Okay."

"Oops! This is my stop! What am I doing just sitting here?" Cooper said after noticing the train was about to depart the 42nd Street station and she needed to change trains here.

"Good luck! I hope you get the job," Josh called out after her just as the doors began to close.

She didn't have time to answer him, so she just turned and waved to him through the window once she was safely on the platform. After Josh and Alex were out of sight, she hurried to catch the train that would take her across town and to her appointment.

When Cooper arrived at the address, she realized it was actually a magazine she had heard of, which was a nice surprise. A lot of jobs she went for were designers whose names weren't familiar to her, and she had to ask Claire, the fashion expert, about them afterward. Others were for products or companies she wasn't totally familiar with, either. A new brand of moisturizer just for teenagers. Fruity-smelling shaving cream meant to appeal to younger buyers. It was amazing the stuff people came up with and the number of models it took to sell it all.

Sitting in the lobby looking at the oversized prints of some of the magazine's covers hanging on the walls made

Cooper a little nervous, and she felt faint flutterings in her stomach. As she continued to look around the room, she noticed there had to be twice as many girls waiting in the lobby as there had been at any of her other appointments. Still, she sat back and tried to relax. She took out her English homework and began looking it over.

An hour later Cooper had run out of homework to do and magazines to read, but the lobby was still just as full because some girls had left, only to be replaced with new ones. She tried to figure out how many girls had arrived after her so she could calculate her wait, but she hadn't paid very close attention when she arrived. Also, a lot of the girls looked the same.

It was 4:30 when Cooper's name was finally called, and she was led down a hallway into an office lined with models' cards. After being introduced to the other two other people in the room and handing the editor a card of her own, Cooper took a seat. And then it hit her. The waves of nausea washed over her, and she felt a headache coming on. It wasn't as bad as the week before, but when she was asked to walk across the room so they could see how she carried herself, Cooper was so dizzy she tripped on the carpeting and almost wasn't able to regain her balance. She wanted to explain that she wasn't feeling well, but that didn't seem very professional. Neither did asking if she could do that part over, so she decided to concentrate really hard on acing the rest of the interview. She held her hair off her face while they took a Polaroid of her and printed her name and the name of her agency on it. Then she sat down carefully, summoning all the poise she could muster as she carefully crossed her legs and sat up extra straight.

After that the questions began: What did she like best

about modeling? How did she get started? What activities was she involved in at school? Cooper managed to keep her mind off her various maladies long enough to come up with at least satisfactory answers. She was even able to paste on a smile while doing so. Until they asked her their final question: What was her last job?

Cooper stammered a little and then finally choked out the brand of jeans her last shoot had been for.

"Wasn't Roelant Guldner the photographer on that one?" the woman who seemed to be running the interview asked.

"Um, yes. He was," Cooper replied in a voice several octaves higher than the one she usually spoke with, making it seem like she'd sucked in a bunch of helium before she answered. She wished the floor would just swallow her up and put her out of her misery. It was taking all of her self-control not to clench her stomach as it cramped up.

"How was he to work with? You're really lucky to get to spend time with someone so talented this early in your career. A lot of girls would kill to have photos of his in their books," a woman who had been silent during the rest of the interview process added.

Those girls can have him, Cooper wanted to say, but she knew there was no way she could. Instead, she took a deep breath and planned to explain, as diplomatically as possible, that it wasn't her favorite shoot.

"I don't think he was at his best the day I worked with him," Cooper began before being interrupted by the phone. She waited for someone in the office to pick it up, but they weren't moving.

Finally one of them said to Cooper, "Is that your phone?"

"Oh my gosh! I guess it is. You see, I just got it and this

is my first call," Cooper explained as she fumbled for the tiny phone in her bag.

"Hello, this is Cooper," she said after finally answering.

"Are you okay? Where are you?" the male voice on the other end of the line asked, his voice filled with concern.

"Excuse me, who is this?"

"It's Josh. Did something happen? Why aren't you home yet?"

"I'm fine, and I really can't talk now," Cooper said much more calmly than she felt. This was worse than if Alex had called her during class! At least that would only mean a detention.

"Okay, but call me as soon as you get home. You had me worried!"

"Fine. I'll talk to you then. Good-bye," Cooper finished, trying to sound as professional as she could under the circumstances. She put the phone away and then began apologizing profusely.

"I'm so sorry for the interruption. I've never had that happen before."

"That's fine. I think we were about done anyway," the leader of the group told her even though they both knew she was just being polite.

Cooper wanted to protest and ask for another chance to prove herself. She really was responsible, she wanted to scream. She'd managed to get herself out of bed on time every day that week without any help from her parents. Didn't that count for anything? But she knew they wouldn't listen, and she really was feeling awful. Also, she wasn't all that anxious to answer any more questions about Roelant Guldner, so she thanked them for their time and quickly left.

She felt better by the time she got off the subway, and

when she arrived home she was almost as good as new. But she'd no sooner dropped her stuff in the entryway when the phone rang. Cooper answered rather tersely, expecting it to be Josh.

"Hello," she said sternly, tapping her foot impatiently while she waited for what she was sure would be an apology.

"Cooper, it's Tara. How'd the interview go? Did they love you?"

"Not exactly," Cooper answered, shifting gears.

"Don't tell me you got sick again," her booking agent moaned.

"Well, I did, but that wasn't the problem, really."

"What was the problem, then, really?" Tara probed.

"They asked me how I liked working with Roelant Guldner—wanting to know all about my last shoot—and then they kept gushing about how wonderful he was and how lucky I was, and I didn't know what to do," Cooper explained. "I wasn't about to lie, but it didn't seem very professional to go into detail about what really happened when we worked together."

"That is a sticky one," Tara agreed. "So what did you say?"

"I didn't get to say much of anything. My cell phone rang, and then they cut the interview short."

"Who was on the phone? I didn't call you. Was it a wrong number? You know, sometimes that happens with new phones."

"It wasn't a wrong number, it was my boyfriend." The word still sounded foreign to Cooper, but she didn't know how else to describe Josh to Tara.

"What? What do you mean it was your boyfriend?"

"I know, I know. But I didn't give him the number. Really!

It was all a big mix-up, and it won't ever happen again."

"It better not," Tara warned. "Now, is that all you have to tell me? No other disasters I should be apprised of?"

"Well, because I was feeling a little dizzy, I tripped while walking across the room for those editors. I'm sure that helped their impression of me."

"Girl, this was just not your day!"

"I know. I don't know what's wrong with me!" Cooper said, a hint of frustration creeping into her voice. "Maybe I need glasses or something?"

"I vote for 'or something.' Now, don't get upset at me for suggesting this, but do you think maybe you're sabotaging yourself on purpose because you're afraid?" Tara suggested. "I could understand it if you were. Your experience at that last shoot was pretty scary."

"I don't know. I hadn't even considered that," Cooper replied honestly.

"How do you feel now?" Tara asked.

"Fine. I felt better on the subway and then fine by the time I got home."

"And were you sick before you got to the appointment?"

"No, not at all. I was perfectly fine," Cooper reported. "So what's your diagnosis, doc?"

"I think you're afraid to get any more jobs because subconsciously you don't want to end up in another bad situation," Tara said.

"Wow! That actually sort of makes sense. I think you're in the wrong line of work," Cooper replied.

"I think I'll stay put for now, no matter how good my diagnosis is. The more important thing is, what are we going to do about this?"

"I don't know. What do you suggest?" Cooper asked.

"I think we need to get you working again as soon as possible. It's like that saying about getting right back on a horse after you fall off. If you wait too long, you may never ride again," Tara explained. "Maybe I can line something up for Friday."

"That would be great, except I'm going out of town on Friday for a week, remember? It's spring break."

"Oh yeah, I remember now. I don't have your schedule in front of me, which is why I forgot for a minute there," Tara said.

"I'm really sorry if that messes up your plans."

"That's okay. Maybe the time away will be good for you. Relax and try to put Roelant Guldner out of your mind. We'll get you back in the saddle as soon as you return."

"Enough with the horseback riding analogies already!" Cooper shouted into the phone. "I'll get over this if only to stop you!"

"Whatever gets results," Tara said. "Enjoy your vacation, and I'll talk to you when you get back."

"I will. Thanks," Cooper replied.

"One more thing. No sunburns! I don't want you coming back to me an ugly, peeling mess," Tara warned.

"I won't. I promise," Cooper vowed. "I'll reapply my sunscreen every hour, on the hour, if it will put your mind at ease."

"It will, thank you very much," Tara said, finally hanging up.

Before grabbing a snack and retreating to her room, Cooper played back the answering machine messages. She wasn't surprised when the first voice she heard was Josh's.

"Cooper, where are you? I thought we were going to do our lab write-ups together. Call me as soon as you get home."

Then, after a beep and a few seconds of nothing, there he was again.

"Cooper, I just talked to you on your cell phone. I'm really sorry if I called at a bad time, but it had been almost three hours and I was worried. I thought something had happened to you since you said you'd only be an hour, so call me when you get this message. I just want to be sure you're all right."

He sounded so forlorn, but Cooper was still mad. Not to mention emotionally drained after her disastrous appointment. She couldn't just not call Josh back, though. That would be rude. So even though she didn't feel prepared for the talk she knew they had to have, Cooper dialed his number.

"Are you home?" Josh asked as soon as Cooper identified herself.

"Yes, and I just got your messages."

"I'm sorry if I interrupted you during your appointment," he apologized again.

"It's just that no one is supposed to call me on that phone except my mom or Tara," Cooper tried to explain. "And I was right in the middle of an interview."

"Oh no," Josh groaned. "I hope I didn't ruin it for you. I'd feel awful if you didn't get the job because of me."

"Don't worry about it. I had already lost the job long before you called."

"Oh. Sorry."

"And I'm sorry for snapping at you. It was just a really bad afternoon, and I've been feeling very pressured, not to mention sick," Cooper told Josh.

"You're not coming down with something right before spring break, are you?" an alarmed Josh asked.

"No. I just felt sick during my appointment. I'm better now."

"Good! Then why don't I come over and we can work on lab write-ups," Josh eagerly suggested.

"You know, I better not. I haven't been home much lately, and I should do some laundry before vacation so I actually have some clothes to take with me. Also, I have geometry that I have to finish, and if you're here I know I won't get it done."

"Are you calling me a distraction?" Josh asked.

"In a word, yes," Cooper replied.

"Well, I'll only agree if you promise to come over here for dinner tomorrow night. My mom invited you. I guess she and my dad want to see who I've been spending all my time with lately."

Cooper already felt ready to fold under the pressure of her failing modeling career and her inability to adjust to being in a relationship, not to mention how far she felt from God these days. Now she had to win over Josh's parents, too? She'd probably spill her milk right in the middle of dinner.

"So what do you say?" Josh persisted when Cooper remained silent.

"I'll be there," she relented.

IN STUDY HALL ON THURSDAY, Cooper finally pulled out her little pocket Bible and the bookmark-sized "Through the Bible in One Year" pamphlet. She hadn't looked at it in over a week and a half, which made her feel horrible, but she'd been using the in-school break to catch up on homework she wasn't getting to because of all the time Josh was taking up in her life now.

As she looked at all the boxes that remained unchecked, Cooper was overwhelmed. *Another thing I'm failing at*, she sighed, then tried to concentrate on the Old Testament passage that was next on the list. She had barely finished one chapter by the time the bell rang. So much for catching up.

In biology class, Mr. Robbins gave the class time to work on their lab write-ups, which was great because it meant less homework for Cooper that night. She was barely going to have time for dinner at Josh's and getting packed for the beach, let alone any unfinished assignments.

With her mind still racing, Cooper suddenly froze in place. Micah, Mr. Robbins' teaching assistant and Cooper's long-time crush, seemed to be staring directly at her. Before she could rub her eyes and look again, though, Josh interrupted.

"This is great! Now we'll have more time to just hang out tonight," Josh said as soon as he and Cooper had pushed their desks together.

"We'll have *some* time," Cooper corrected. "Remember, we're leaving right after school tomorrow, which means I have to go home and pack tonight."

"I thought you did that last night?"

"No, I did laundry so I'm ready to pack," Cooper explained.

"Oh, I didn't realize they were two separate jobs."

"Well, they are."

"I don't know why you can't just throw a few things in a duffel bag," Josh told her. "It's just the beach. How much stuff do you need?"

"You'd be surprised," Cooper said before settling in and getting to work on their assignment.

It took the rest of the hour to finish up, but they did, explaining in great detail the insides of a crayfish and what they had learned from cutting up his poor little body.

"My mom would not be happy about that assignment at all," Josh said as he and Cooper raced toward the cafeteria and the notoriously long Coke-machine line.

"Why?" Cooper asked, not understanding.

"She won't even shop anywhere that sells live lobster. You know, like in those tanks with their claws all rubber-banded together?" he explained. "And those are at least going to be eaten. In the lab, we're just cutting the little creatures up to poke around at their insides before throwing them away."

"It does sound really gross when you put it that way," Cooper agreed, then added, "So I guess it's safe to assume shellfish won't be on the menu at your house tonight?"

"It's safe to say that. Actually, I convinced my mom to do the cooking so you don't have to suffer through one of my dad's creations. It's bizarre, but he can take one of Mom's recipes and use the exact same ingredients she does and it will come out completely inedible. I don't know how he does it."

"Thanks for the warning," Cooper said. "Now we better hurry." With that, she took off at a sprint for her locker to grab her lunch box before meeting up with Josh again by the cafeteria entrance.

Claire and Alex were waiting at the Coke machine, quarters in hand, and Cooper and Josh tried to say "hi" but were both out of breath from their little workout. You weren't really supposed to run in the halls of Hudson High, but as long as you were hurrying to get somewhere instead of just playing around, teachers were more forgiving. If she had to walk, Cooper wouldn't make it to the cafeteria until lunch was half over!

Once the foursome was settled in the courtyard and Cooper had a mouthful of peanut butter and jelly, Alex said, "Why didn't you answer your phone?"

"When? Last night? It didn't ring," Cooper replied, still a bit confused.

"No, during English! I called you on your cell phone and you didn't pick up!"

"You did not!" Cooper charged. "I thought I warned you about that."

"Is that why you didn't answer?" Alex grinned mischievously.

"No. I didn't answer because I had it turned off. I'm not going to willingly give you an opportunity to humiliate me."

"That's fine, because I didn't call you anyway," Alex admitted. "I was only joking. I wouldn't really get you in trouble in class, I just like to make you *think* I would. Besides, you said the phone was just for work, and despite what you might think, I'm not a total jerk. I do actually listen, so you don't have to tell me everything twice."

"I appreciate that," Cooper said, careful not to look in Josh's direction. Would he feel like Alex was implying *he* was a jerk because he *hadn't* taken her warning seriously not to call her on that phone? Worse yet, might Josh think she had told Alex about the phone fiasco from the day before and assume his dig was deliberate? When they walked to class together after lunch, Cooper couldn't tell for sure what Josh was thinking. He seemed a little quiet, but not necessarily upset. And when he said good-bye to her at her classroom door, he smiled like he always did. That seemed like a good sign, and Cooper decided to try not to read too much into something that might not even be there.

❋   ❋   ❋

"So I should be there at 5:30?" Cooper asked Josh before he left her to catch the subway home after reading group.

"Yeah. My parents get home around 4:30 because they have to be at school so early, so we usually eat by 6:00," Josh explained.

"Okay, I'll see you then," Cooper promised.

"You have the directions I gave you, right?"

"Yep," she replied, pulling a piece of notebook paper from her pocket and waving it at him.

"Bye, then," Josh called to her and Claire after he and Alex had already begun moving toward the 72nd Street station.

"So you're going to meet his parents? That's so romantic!" Claire gushed as soon as Josh was out of sight.

"What's romantic about it? I think it's scary," Cooper admitted.

"He wants his parents to meet you, which means he must really, really like you a lot," Claire explained.

"Or they just want to make sure they approve of me before they let Josh come to the beach with us," Cooper suggested, opting for a decidedly more negative scenario than her optimistic friend.

"Are you nervous they're not going to like you?" Claire finally asked.

"Of course I am," Cooper answered without even stopping to consider the question. "I mean, Josh and I don't even seem to really have all the kinks in our relationship worked out, and now this might be just one more thing that could be a problem."

"How could his parents be a problem?"

"If they don't like me, I guess," Cooper admitted with a shrug.

"How could they not like you?" Claire asked with the sincerity of a best friend.

Those words melted away almost all of Cooper's apprehension. "Thanks," Cooper said.

"So what are you going to wear?"

"I don't know. I've never had to pick out an outfit to meet my boyfriend's parents before."

"If you need any help, just give me a call. You know I'm always happy to come to the rescue where clothes are concerned," Claire generously offered.

"I may be calling you frantically in an hour," Cooper promised as the elevator deposited Claire on her floor.

There wasn't much time to worry about meeting anyone's parents once Cooper got home. She had promised her mother the night before that she would clean her room before going to Josh's so it wouldn't be a mess over spring break. She knew bringing a crane in to clear the area was out of the question, even though it would have made things much easier. Instead, Cooper dove in herself, sorting piles and piling sorted items and making an even bigger mess in the process.

Nearly an hour later, though, all the clean clothes were where they belonged, the dirty ones she hadn't gotten to the night before were actually in the hamper, and all the surfaces that were supposed to be seen were visible—including the floor, desk, and bed.

Her thoroughness in one area meant she would have to skimp in another, though. It was almost 5:00 when she finished. She only had ten minutes before she had to leave for Josh's house, and she was a mess after her little cleaning binge. There wasn't even time to call Claire to ask for help. Instead, Cooper ran into the bathroom to wash her face and brush her teeth, then ran back to her room, peeling off her dirty clothes as she went. Putting them where they belonged so she didn't mess up her clean room took a few more seconds than leaving them on the floor would have, but being able to find what she wanted to wear without having to dig through endless piles saved her time, so it all evened out.

After choosing a pair of black pants, her dressier black boots, and a cobalt blue fitted dress shirt—which she loved because it made her steely-gray eyes look even more intense—Cooper raced back into the bathroom to brush her hair before pulling it up in a twist with a few wisps falling out. Now all that was left was her makeup, and she had just two minutes to go. She started by brushing on a light dusting of loose powder and then added a bit of gray pencil to her eyes. She brushed her eyebrows, applied a single coat of mascara, and then, for her big finish, swiped some rosy gloss across her lips. Some citrus body spray finished up the rest of her, and she grabbed her black leather jacket and her backpack and was out the door.

She was still buttoning the cuffs of her shirt in the elevator on her way to the lobby, but at least she was on time. The subways would be crowded since it was rush hour, and she didn't want that to make her late.

She wasn't. The subways were fine, the directions were good, and at 5:29 she found herself standing on what she was relatively certain was Josh's stoop. She took a deep breath, went inside, and found his apartment right there on the first floor. His building was much smaller than Cooper's and without a doorman. Instead, it looked like an old house that had been divided up into apartments. Also, Cooper noticed it was a "walk-up," which was a nice way of saying there was no elevator. But it was a charming building, unlike her own modern, nondescript one.

"You must be Cooper!" a woman with long, dark hair and kind, crinkly eyes said as she swung the door open.

"Um, yes, I am," Cooper agreed unnecessarily.

"Come in, come in!" she said, ushering Cooper into a cozy but colorful living room. As soon as the door was shut, she called out down the hall, "Josh, your guest is here."

"I'm Sarah Trobisch," the woman who Cooper could only assume was Josh's mom said. "Now, come sit down and tell me all about yourself."

Talk about pressure! Panic filled Cooper at the thought of being grilled to find out if she was good enough to be Josh's girlfriend, but Mrs. Trobisch put her instantly at ease. She had on a flowing gauze dress with an African print, and her feet, which she tucked under herself when she sat down, were bare. The front of her hair was pulled back gently and held in a loose knot by a pair of red chopsticks.

"If you could travel anywhere in the world, where would be the first place you'd visit?" Cooper was asked. She'd been expecting something about school or grades or what her parents did, so this really threw her for a loop.

"Mom! You're not quizzing her already, are you? You could at least wait until dinner, when she can pretend her mouth is full so she won't have to answer," Josh said, entering the airy, light-filled room.

"I wasn't grilling," Mrs. Trobisch countered. "Cooper and I were merely getting to know each other."

"That's what I'm afraid of!" Josh said before adding, "Has she met Dad yet?"

"No, she just got here. He's in the kitchen, though, and I know he can't wait to meet her."

"The kitchen? You left Dad in the kitchen with the food?" Josh said, obviously alarmed.

"Don't worry! It's just the salad. He can't possibly mess it up," Mrs. Trobisch said calmly. "I'm not even letting him make the dressing."

"Good!" Josh replied.

"Are you finally going to say hello to your guest now that you're done accusing me of tormenting the company and your father of sabotaging the meal?"

"Hi, Cooper," Josh responded. "Did you find the place okay?"

"No problem. It's funny—I know Claire and I have walked through this neighborhood dozens of times, and I'm sure I've come right past your house without ever knowing you lived here."

"Now the next time you pass by you'll have to stop in," Josh's mother suggested. "Even if this one isn't home," she added, motioning to Josh.

"I'd like that," Cooper said, then thought, *This whole meeting-the-parents thing isn't a big deal at all.*

"Come on," Josh motioned to her. "I'll introduce you to my dad and make sure he's staying focused only on the salad."

Cooper followed Josh into the kitchen, which was painted bright red. There were rough-hewn beams stretching across the ceiling with baskets and dried flowers and herbs hanging from them, and the table was a matching slab of dark wood surrounded by a bunch of mismatched chairs. A collection of other baskets and wooden bowls were displayed on the wall, and the tile counter tops were cluttered with appliances, brightly colored pottery, and pretty glass jars filled with various liquids. Her mother would have hated the clutter, Cooper knew, but she loved the claustrophobic feel of it all. Nothing was ever left sitting out at the Ellis home, while here it seemed everything was.

"Dad, this is Cooper Ellis," Josh said to a tall man with brown hair the exact shade as his own. At that, he turned around suddenly, causing an avocado to roll on the floor.

After retrieving the escaped vegetable, Mr. Trobisch reached out his hand to shake Cooper's, then immediately pulled it back. She wondered if it was some kind of a trick, but then he reached for a nearby dish towel, wiped his hand thoroughly, and offered it again.

"Sorry about that, but I figured you'd like your tomato juice in a glass, not on your hand," he said with a smile.

"You're right about that," Cooper agreed, smiling back.

"Dinner will be ready in about ten minutes," Josh's mom announced, appearing behind them. "Do you want to show Cooper the rest of the house before we eat?"

"How about a guided tour?" Josh asked.

"Sure," Cooper replied gamely.

The rest of the house was much the same as the rooms Cooper had entered first. A lot of bright Indian prints and big, squishy cushions with collections displayed on shelves, walls, and tables—anywhere there was a flat surface.

When they got to Josh's room, Cooper wasn't even surprised by the fact that his walls were deep, rusty orange. He had a batik print blanket on his bed, his guitar leaning against the wall in one corner, and wooden crates stacked up at different angles to make a bookcase. Against another wall was a really old refrigerator.

"Is that just in case you get hungry in the middle of the night and are too lazy to go to the kitchen for a snack?" Cooper joked, motioning toward the antique appliance.

"It was my grandparents'. Actually, this whole place was. When they died they left it to my parents, but we used to rent it out because Mom and Dad didn't want to raise us in the city. When my older brother went off to college, though, they changed their minds. They were tired of commuting from Staten Island."

"That still doesn't completely explain why the fridge is in your room," Cooper pointed out.

"Oh yeah. I guess I got sidetracked," Josh said. "It doesn't work anymore, and my parents were going to get rid of it, so I drug it in here. I keep my stereo inside and all my CDs," he explained, pulling the door open to show Cooper exactly what he meant.

"That is so cool!"

"Of course, the speakers aren't in there or you wouldn't hear anything," he added.

"Of course," Cooper agreed.

"So what do you think?" he finally asked, as if he had been holding back from doing so earlier.

"About the stereo, your house, or your parents?" Cooper asked.

"Any of it. All of it. Whatever," Josh tried to clarify.

Cooper quickly delivered her verdict: "Your parents are so great and so is this house! Why don't we ever hang out over here?"

"I didn't know you'd want to," Josh answered honestly.

"Of course I would. We all would. I love this place."

"I'm just never sure," Josh continued. "Especially when I'm with all of you. I feel like I'm in the way sometimes. Like you and Alex and Claire all speak some secret language that only the three of you know, and there's no translation book available."

"What do you mean?" Cooper asked, taken aback by his admission. She thought she was the only one feeling growing pains as their relationship evolved, but it seemed like they had more problems to work out than she thought.

Just as they were about to begin hashing it out, though, Josh's mom called them to dinner. Apparently, the problem-solving would have to wait.

DINNER WITH JOSH'S PARENTS would have been wonderful if Cooper hadn't been so concerned about the talk she knew needed to be continued after the meal. As it was, the manicotti shells filled with cheese and covered with tomato sauce were delicious, the salad perfectly chopped, despite Josh's worries, and Mr. and Mrs. Trobisch amazingly nice.

Instead of treating Cooper like a kid and asking her what she wanted to be when she grew up or talking to her only about her classes at school, they treated her like she was already an adult, an equal. They seemed genuinely interested in what she thought and listened carefully to the things she had to say, even if she was just talking about her favorite place in Central Park or her neighborhood.

Afterward, Josh's mom set a dish of vanilla ice cream in front of each of them. At least, Cooper thought it was ice cream, but Josh's protests to his mother revealed the truth.

"You know, Mom, some people might not like tofu for dessert," Josh suggested. Before she could respond, he turned to Cooper and confessed, "You have to watch her or she'll try to feed you soy milk ice cream or some other kind with tofu in it."

"It's not soy milk this time," his mother corrected, "so

don't go poisoning Cooper against my dessert unfairly. I remembered that you didn't like that when I bought it before, so this time I got goat's milk ice cream."

"Oh, I'm sure that will put her mind at ease," Josh teased.

"She'll love it," Mrs. Trobisch predicted.

Cooper just sat quietly, taking it all in. She hadn't ever had goat's milk before, but she knew she didn't like goat cheese—it was so strong. She didn't see any way out of at least tasting the dessert, though. She was a guest, after all.

"If you don't like it you don't have to finish it," Mr. Trobisch offered as Cooper raised her first spoonful to her mouth.

It was a sweet gesture, but Cooper knew she couldn't just try one bite and put her spoon down. She would have to eat at least the majority of the rather large scoop she'd been given, regardless of the taste. With that in mind and all eyes on her, Cooper took a bite. She was willing her face to remain emotionless no matter what message her taste buds sent, which is why she was surprised when she felt her mouth curl into a smile.

"This is delicious!" she said enthusiastically before devouring another spoonful.

"Thank you," Mrs. Trobisch replied triumphantly, then she immediately shot her husband and son a smug look of victory.

"She's just being polite," Josh chimed in.

"No, I'm not," Cooper said, jumping to the defense of herself and her dessert. "It's really good! I've never had ice cream that was so . . . well, creamy!" she finished after searching for just the right adjective.

"If you want some more when you finish that, just say so," Josh's mom added. "There's plenty left over."

"Now you're just showing off," Josh accused.

The teasing continued through doing the dishes, which Cooper insisted on helping with, partly because she knew she should and partly because she was trying to put off the confrontation she and Josh had unofficially scheduled. No matter how slow she washed, though, eventually all the dishes were clean and put away.

"I think I'm going to walk Cooper partway home," Josh announced.

"Do you have to leave already?" Mrs. Trobisch asked. "It feels like you just got here."

"I still have to pack for the beach, so I really should," Cooper explained. She didn't add that she also had a more pressing engagement with Josh, even though that was really why she was hurrying out the door.

"We enjoyed meeting you," Mrs. Trobisch said, clasping Cooper's hand. "You're a lovely girl. It's too bad we didn't get to see you before the dance. I bet you looked simply magical."

"Thank you," Cooper answered politely.

"I tried to persuade Josh to take a camera, but he absolutely refused."

"Oh, my parents took rolls and rolls of pictures. I'm sure my mom can part with some."

"That would be wonderful, but only if you're sure she won't mind."

"She won't," Cooper assured Josh's mom. "I think she got triple prints or something crazy like that. There are plenty to go around. I'll try to dig some up and give them to Josh to bring to you."

"I'll look forward to seeing them."

"Good night, then," Cooper called from the entryway.

"Good night," Josh's mom and dad echoed back.

❈   ❈   ❈

"So back to this secret language you mentioned," Cooper said as she and Josh headed up Fifth Avenue in the direction she lived. Her apartment building was about forty blocks away, and the subway station wasn't going to be on this street. But it felt good to walk, at least for a while, as it meant Cooper didn't have to look directly at Josh while they talked.

"Maybe it's not a secret language," Josh admitted. "It's more like a secret club."

"Oh, that makes me feel much better," Cooper joked, but when Josh didn't laugh she asked, "What do you mean? Give me an example."

"Every time I'm with you guys is an example!" Josh wailed.

"I don't understand," Cooper said sadly.

"Take last weekend," Josh began. "We went downtown to watch that movie being filmed."

"But you're the one who promised we'd do whatever he wanted," Cooper pointed out, her voice filled with frustration.

"It wasn't that Alex picked how we spent our afternoon; it's how your plans all seem to tie in together without you even having to discuss it. The movie set is by the store *Claire* wanted to go to, which just happens to be by *your* favorite bagel place. You're all even hungry for the same food at the same time!"

"But I had nothing to do with that!" Cooper protested before reminding, "And I went with you to get pizza."

"I know, but even then I felt like you'd rather be with Claire looking at Shaun Cassidy books and reminiscing about

The Hardy Boys. Like I was tearing you away from your friends."

"Please know that I would never rather be looking at Shaun Cassidy books than hanging out with you," Cooper tried to assure Josh. "I don't know what else I can do to fix this, though."

"I don't think there's anything you can do. That's what I'm saying. None of you do it on purpose; it just happens. You have this shared history and all these memories together, and I can't compete with that."

"But it's not a competition," Cooper protested.

"Sometimes it feels like it is, like I'm competing with Claire and Alex for your attention," Josh admitted. "That's why I've been trying to spend more time alone with you, but it seems like you're busy a lot."

"I'm not busy a lot. In fact, I spend a ton of my time with you. But I have to admit I'm feeling a little overwhelmed. I love being with you, but my homework is suffering, my quiet time is nonexistent, and I never have any time to myself."

"So what are you saying? You want to break up?" Josh asked a little angrily.

"No. That's not what I'm saying at all. We just need to figure out some sort of balance. I can't stop spending time with Claire and Alex, and you don't want to spend a lot of time with me when they're around, too. But I also have work and school and my family. My parents haven't said anything, but I've barely been home lately, either, so it's just a matter of time before they bring that up. I don't know how to fit it all in."

"I don't, either," Josh said, sounding disappointed. "And I can't help noticing that everything and everyone else has seniority over me."

"Seniority?" Cooper questioned.

"Yeah, seniority. I was the last thing added to that list, so it doesn't seem too unreasonable for me to be afraid I'll be the first to go if you decide you have too much going on."

"You make it sound like I'm cleaning out my closet and you're a sweater I'm going to send to Goodwill."

"Maybe I am," Josh said. "I mean, if the sweater fits, or in this case doesn't . . ."

"I can't believe you think I'd do that!" an offended Cooper said.

"How can I be sure you won't?" Josh asked, looking at Cooper for the first time in blocks.

She stopped walking and looked into Josh's eyes. "I guess you can't," she shrugged. "But on the other hand, I can't be sure you won't decide you'd rather have another sweater, either."

"You're the only sweater I want," Josh said, smiling at last and taking Cooper's hand in his.

"Good. Now we just have to find a way to work all this other stuff out," Cooper decided.

"And how do you propose we do that?"

"I have absolutely no idea," Cooper admitted.

"Maybe we can come up with some solutions at the beach," Josh suggested.

"That would be great," Cooper agreed. "And 1 promise I'll try to be more sensitive to how you feel when we're with Claire and Alex, but I'm warning you that on vacation together it's going to be hard to *not* be with Claire and Alex."

"I get it," Josh acknowledged. "And I'll try to be more understanding, too."

"Think of it this way," Cooper suggested. "The more time you spend with all three of us, the more shared memories we'll have that will include you."

"You have a point there."

"So are we going to walk all the way to my house or are we going to get on the subway at some point?" Cooper finally asked.

"We only have twelve more blocks to go," Josh said after looking up at the street signs to figure out where they were. "We might as well just keep walking, don't you think?"

"Fine with me," Cooper agreed.

And they were a wonderful twelve blocks. Josh was holding Cooper's hand, the weather was warm, and there were even a few stars out. By the time they reached Cooper's building it seemed like nothing could get to her. She had a great boyfriend—whose parents seemed to like her—she had great friends, and tomorrow was spring break. No school or teachers or homework for a whole week. Just sun and water and relaxation. She was invincible.

❋ ❋ ❋

"I'm home," Cooper called out as she entered the apartment.

"Down here, honey," her mother called.

"Sorry I'm a little late, but Josh and I walked home," Cooper called back as she followed the voice. It was like an above-water game of Marco Polo.

"That's fine as long as you still have time to pack," Mrs. Ellis replied.

By now Cooper had reached her mother's voice. She was about to reach out and tag her and say "You're it" and then declare herself the winner of the game, but instead she just stood in the doorway of her bedroom and stared.

"Wha-what are you doing?" Cooper asked even though she knew the answer before the question was out of her mouth.

"I'm just measuring a few things for your new room," her mother explained as Cooper watched her scurry around with a note pad and a pen, making little notations.

So the plan was still in place. Just as Cooper was getting her life straightened out, it seemed her mother was going to turn her world upside down.

THE ENTIRE SCHOOL seemed to hum with excitement on Friday. Frustrated teachers were throwing out their lesson plans, realizing there was no way they were going to get any work out of students whose bodies may still have been present but whose minds had left on vacation long before the final bell rang.

Even Cooper was caught up in the excitement. She was feeling much more hopeful about how their week at the beach was going to turn out, especially after her talk last night with Josh. A fun-filled week with friends and, more important, without school. That couldn't possibly be bad, Cooper reasoned as she struggled to cram all of her books in her locker. She wasn't taking a single one of them home over the holiday, and it felt great.

She hurriedly slammed shut the metal door before everything came tumbling back out, then turned around and leaned against the locker for added insurance it was latched. As she was leaning there waiting for Claire and Josh and Alex, the weirdest thing happened. Micah Jacobson walked by, which wasn't weird in and of itself. What was weird was that he stopped right in front of Cooper and spoke to her! It was a good thing she was already propped up against something or she might have toppled right over from the shock of it all.

"So . . . any big plans for break, Ellis?" he asked, moving closer so they didn't have students walking in between them while they talked.

"Just, uh, going to the Hamptons," she replied, trying not to choke on her tongue.

"That's cool," he answered. Then, without waiting for Cooper to ask, he volunteered, "I'm going to Florida. I'm still deciding between a couple of colleges. I'm going to look at one of them again, and I figure I can check out some of the local bands at the same time."

"Sounds good," Cooper said for lack of a more original observation to share. She knew that the second Micah walked away she would think of a million things she wanted to say to him, but now while she had the chance her mind was completely blank.

"Oh, there's Jim, I gotta go," Micah announced, motioning to one of his band mates who was rapidly approaching. Before leaving, though, he turned back to Cooper and said, "Don't have too much fun without me."

"I . . . uh . . . I won't," Cooper stammered, but by the time she got the jumbled words out he was already gone.

She was still standing there in a daze when Josh approached.

"Can you believe we got out of class late on the last day of school before spring break?" he asked her.

"Bummer," Cooper replied, forcing herself back to reality. "All we had to do was complete a work sheet and grade one another's papers, then we were free to go."

"That figures. I guess there's no use complaining about it

now, though, because in just a few short hours we'll be at the beach."

"That's right!" Alex shouted, coming up behind the couple and surprising them. "The sun and the sand are calling my name. What are you guys waiting for?"

"We're waiting for Claire," Cooper reminded. "You do remember her, don't you? Dark hair? Puts up with a lot from you? Is any of this ringing a bell?"

"Hmmm. She sounds vaguely familiar," Alex said, stroking his chin and pretending to think really hard about it.

"Here I am; we can go now," Claire said as she came rushing toward the group. Cooper waited for her to offer an explanation about where she had been, but she didn't. Instead, she stowed her notebook in her locker right next to Cooper's and headed for the door. It seemed there was nothing to do but follow her.

"Alex, where's your stuff?" Cooper asked as soon as they were out on the street and truly free at last.

"Everything I need is right in here," Alex replied, patting his not exactly overstuffed backpack.

"Whatever you say." Cooper shook her head at her friend and wondered not for the first time about his personal hygiene.

"What about Josh? He has less stuff than I do," Alex pointed out smugly.

"That's because he dropped his duffel bag off at my house this morning before school," Cooper explained just as smugly.

Alex wasn't fazed, though. Instead, he just said, "Good, that means I'll have someone to borrow clothes from when all of my stuff gets dirty."

"Which will be when? Tomorrow?" Claire interjected.

"Very funny," Alex shot back.

"Okay, guys, we'd better speed it up or we're going to get left behind. I promised my parents we'd be home right after school. And if I know my mother, she'll have the rental van all loaded up by now and will be waiting down on the street for us."

"Forward march, then. Let's get moving, troops!" Alex ordered. "I don't want to miss the Ellis express."

❊   ❊   ❊

"There you kids are," Mrs. Ellis said as soon as the foursome turned the corner.

As Cooper predicted, the van was loaded with supplies, including enough food for them to stay for an entire month. Her suitcase was in there, too, as was Josh's bag, and in a matter of minutes all eight passengers were on board and the van was speeding toward the Long Island Expressway.

"The L.I.E. is going to be horrible by this time, so I hope you're all comfortable," Mr. Ellis announced shortly after the trip was underway. They weren't even to midtown yet, and there were cars everywhere. Cooper couldn't figure out who drove in New York, aside from cabbies and delivery people. Her parents didn't have a car and neither did Claire's. You could take a cab just about anywhere in the city for less than what it would cost to park once you drove there, and if you wanted off-the-street parking like you could get in her building, Cooper had heard her parents say it was almost as much as renting another small apartment. But obviously people did it, because when Cooper looked out the windows on either side of the van, there were cars pressing in.

"Should we turn the radio on?" Mr. Hughes asked, to

which a resounding chorus of "yes" emerged from the back half of the van.

"Why don't you see if you can find some traffic information," Mr. Ellis suggested, which resulted in the cheers turning to boos.

Cooper, sitting next to Josh in the very back seat, leaned her head on his shoulder as her dad continued to maneuver through the bumper-to-bumper traffic. It had been a long and eventful week, and she was looking forward to a good night's sleep after a relaxing walk along the ocean.

The next thing she heard was "We're here, Cooper. Wake up and enjoy your vacation."

She opened her sleepy eyes and looked up to see Josh looking down at her. She had fallen asleep and missed the entire trip! She hoped she hadn't drooled or snored or anything else embarrassing. She'd have to ask Claire later when they were alone.

"Let's get everything inside and unpacked before anyone takes off exploring," Mrs. Hughes suggested and Mrs. Ellis eagerly seconded.

Cooper grabbed her bag and handed Josh his, and they each hauled a bag of groceries, as well.

"Be careful, I think you have the eggs in that one, Cooper," her mother warned, startling her still-drowsy daughter and causing her to lose her tentative grip on the sack. As she did, the eggs went crashing to the ground, where they landed with an unceremonious thud.

"That was my birthday cake, wasn't it?" Cooper asked her mother, referring to the chocolate angel food she had requested.

"I'm sure we can get another dozen eggs, but they'll cost a small fortune here on the island."

"Sorry," Cooper meekly said. "I guess I wasn't all the way awake yet."

"That's all right, honey. But why don't you run inside and get some damp paper towels so we can get it cleaned up. We don't want dried egg on the sidewalk all week."

As she entered the beach house, the scent of musty wood and sand and salt water mixed with some sort of floral scent immediately took Cooper back to previous vacations. The furnishings were just the same: a lot of blue and cranberry tones, with big floral print overstuffed chairs, crisp striped curtains, comfy nooks, and a pillow-filled window seat. She was so busy looking around that Cooper almost forgot for a minute that she was on a mission.

It was amazing how quickly everything was unpacked. Less than thirty minutes after arriving, Cooper, Josh, Claire, and Alex were standing on the shore watching the calm surf roll in as the sun sank in the sky.

"I can't believe you didn't invite me last year," Alex complained to the girls.

"Be good or we won't invite you *next* year," Cooper warned.

"Your mom will," Alex stated confidently. "I'm like the son she never had."

"I don't think I'd go quite that far. What do you think, Claire?" asked Cooper.

"Oh no you don't! I'm staying out of this one."

"Chicken," Cooper teased before running into the waves and splashing at her friend.

Before long they were all soaked and had to waddle back up to the house. They had been so anxious to get out on the beach that they hadn't even changed out of their clothes from school, which meant they were all wearing pants that now clung to their calves.

Cooper was trying to wring out her pant legs but not having much success. She knew she had to at least make the effort, though, or her mother would chastise her for dripping water all over the house.

"This sand sure is itchy," she pointed out before opening the back door.

"Yeah, I'll remind you of that the next time you want to run in the water fully clothed and take all of us with you," Josh said.

❋   ❋   ❋

"How about another hamburger, Alex?" Mrs. Ellis offered.

"Have you guys picked up on how it works here yet? Dad's in charge of the grill, but Mom is in charge of making sure you guys overeat," Cooper explained to Josh and Alex.

"See," Alex whispered to Cooper. "What did I tell you? The son she never had."

Cooper just rolled her eyes. She noticed that Josh had noticed her and Alex sharing a secret, though, and immediately felt guilty. Was this one of those moments where he felt like an outsider? And if it was, what could she have done to stop Alex from whispering something to her?

"Who's up for s'mores?" Mrs. Hughes asked as she came out onto the patio wielding shish kebab skewers and a big bag of marshmallows.

"Count me in," Cooper said eagerly, reaching for the bag.

After the ingredients had been handed out, the adults moved their party inside, where the seats were more cushioned and the bugs weren't as apt to be biting.

Sitting so close to the ocean like this in the evening was Cooper's favorite part of vacation. Her whole body relaxed as she looked up at the stars while the water sang her a lullaby and the outdoorsy smell of a campfire filled her nostrils. It was enough to make her want to move away from the city permanently. She knew, though, that if she did she'd eventually miss the sounds of the sirens and car alarms and stray cats that sang her to sleep in Manhattan just as much as she missed this between vacations.

"Does anyone want to go for a walk?" Alex asked after everyone had eaten their fill of the marshmallow, chocolate, and graham cracker sandwiches.

Claire was up and ready to go in an instant. "I could use a little exercise," she said, doing a few lunges to stretch her legs in preparation.

"I don't think I can stand, let alone walk," Josh admitted, patting his bulging stomach.

"I'll stay behind, too," Cooper agreed, remembering her and Josh's talk and knowing it might be one of the only times they would be alone together all week.

"So what do you want to do?" Josh asked.

"How about we just stare at the stars?" Cooper suggested. "But let's go sit on the beach. I love to be able to run my fingers and toes through the sand."

"Sounds good, assuming I can get up from this chair," Josh agreed.

Cooper hopped up and then held a helping hand out to Josh, pulling him up from his seat.

"This is much better," Cooper said, sighing contentedly, once they had both plopped down on the strip of narrow beach that was directly in front of the house they were staying in. From where they sat, Cooper could see the lights burning in the living room as her parents and Claire's caught up.

She wondered if she and Claire and Alex would sit around like that one day with their spouses while their kids walked on the beach. It was hard to imagine ever being that old. It was also hard for Cooper to imagine where Josh fit into her little what-if scenario, and it took too much brain power to think about it right now. Instead, she lay back on the sand and stretched out her arms and legs, then began flapping them gently.

"What are you doing?" Josh asked, looking at her as if she had suddenly lost her mind.

"I'm making sand angels," she replied seriously. "Don't tell me you've never done it."

"That's exactly what I'm telling you."

"Well, give it a try. Now's your chance."

"I think I'll pass," Josh said in a firm but nice way that let Cooper know there was no way he would be joining her any time soon, but he didn't want to ruin her fun, either.

"Do you know anything about the constellations?" Cooper asked Josh a few minutes later.

"Sorry, I don't."

"Good, then you can play," she told him. "All you have to do is lay your head back in the sand so you're staring straight up at the sky."

"My hair will get all full of sand," he complained.

"You're at the beach. You're supposed to be covered in sand."

Josh finally gave in. "Okay, now what do I do?" he asked once he was reclining on a lumpy sand pillow.

"You look for pictures in the stars."

"Pictures of what?"

"Anything," Cooper told him. "It's like that game where you study the clouds and try to find things in them."

"So why can't I know anything about astronomy in order to play?"

"Because then you try to see what you're supposed to see instead of what your imagination wants to see," Cooper explained.

"In other words, big dippers and little dippers aren't allowed?"

"Exactly."

After spotting a dog, a sea monkey, a toaster, and Mr. Peanut all residing together in the night sky, Cooper and Josh decided to call it a day.

"Thanks for staying here with me," Josh said once he and Cooper were back on the deck of the beach house. He even gave her shoulder a little squeeze when he said it, banishing all her fears that the week was going to be a difficult one because he and Alex were on hand. With his arm around her shoulder, she had trouble remembering why she had been worried in the first place.

"You're welcome. I had a really great time," Cooper said, looking up into Josh's face.

"It means a lot to me that you picked me over Alex and Claire," Josh added.

Suddenly, Cooper was speechless. She wished she could rewind that last moment and return to when things were perfect. To find out that Josh really saw their time together as a popularity contest pierced Cooper right through the heart. She thought they were getting past this.

"What?" Josh finally asked after Cooper was silent a little too long. "What's wrong?"

"Didn't you listen to anything I said last night?" Cooper

asked, taking a step backward and out of Josh's grasp.

"Of course I did."

"Then I don't understand why you think I picked you over Claire and Alex. I've picked *all of you*. You're all in my life."

"I know," Josh said soothingly as he moved closer to touch Cooper's arm. "I just said I was glad that you chose to stay behind with me tonight. What's wrong with that?"

"Nothing tonight. But what happens tomorrow night when I choose to go for a walk instead? Do I have to worry that you'll be upset because you weren't 'chosen' that time?"

"I don't know," Josh admitted.

"I think you'd better figure it out," Cooper replied.

DESPITE THE ROCKY START, the week flew by. Cooper tried her best to divide her time fairly between everyone, which made her feel a bit like a wishbone, but she didn't know what else to do. Aside from those worries, the days were carefree, punctuated mainly by meals, with dinner always being cooked over an open flame. Cooper and the others splashed in the water and explored the beach and lay in the sand in between. By Friday they had even developed a routine. They would all rise and throw on their bathing suits before breakfast, then hit the beach with their stomachs still full of cereal or breakfast burritos or bagels and cream cheese. Lunch would draw them back to the house, and then it was back to the sand for a game of Frisbee or paddle ball, which Cooper always lost. Then around 3:00 they would go inside and shower before walking into town for ice cream at Rod's Drive-In, which wasn't a drive-in at all but an old-fashioned soda fountain. Cooper's order changed each day from a vanilla Coke to a chocolate malt, then back again, and she didn't know how she was going to live without those afternoon snacks when she went back to Manhattan.

"I'm so glad Greg introduced us to Rod's last year," Claire

said as the gang and their full stomachs made their way back to the beach house.

"I know," Cooper agreed. "I wonder why he isn't here this year?"

"Who's Greg?" Josh asked.

"His parents own the blue house next to ours," Cooper explained. "He lives on the Upper East Side and goes to some snooty prep school, but he's not like that at all."

"Cooper's right," Claire nodded. "He rescued us last year by showing us where to go in town and what parts of the beach to avoid. He even took us out to a movie after we had trouble finding the theater by ourselves."

"So what did you do to chase him away?" Alex asked. "We could use another guy around here to balance out you girls with all your jewelry-making and putting on makeup to go to the beach."

"Oh, give me a break," Cooper countered. "We strung beads and made earrings *one* night, and we offered to make you a manly looking choker but you turned us down. Now, as for wearing makeup to the beach, it was just a little water-proof mascara. Let it go."

"Today it's waterproof mascara, tomorrow you'll be having your lipstick and eyeliner tattooed on like that lady I saw on TV," Alex dramatically predicted.

"You are so bizarre" was Cooper's only response.

❋   ❋   ❋

"So what are you men throwing on the barbecue to-night?" Cooper asked when she found her dad and Mr. Hughes on the back patio with several bags of food.

"Oh, that's a surprise," he answered mysteriously. "I

could tell you, but then I'd have to kill you."

"I don't think I want to know quite that bad, but thanks."

"How about a little volleyball before dinner?" Alex suggested, grabbing the ball from a basket full of sports equipment that came with the house.

Cooper looked to Josh to try to gauge his interest before answering. He'd been awfully quiet on the walk back from Rod's, and she was wondering what had upset him this time. Before she could figure it out, Josh answered for both of them.

"We'd love to. Come on, Cooper."

Soon they were involved in an intense game. So intense they didn't notice they were being watched until a voice said, "Aren't you ever going to let me rotate in? I've been sitting here on the bench forever."

"Greg!" Cooper and Claire screamed in unison.

"We were just talking about you," Claire told him, giving their sandy-haired friend a hug.

"When did you get here?" Cooper excitedly asked.

"Just now. Our school has its break next week, so we left right after I got out today."

"That's too bad. We're going back Sunday right after church," Claire explained.

"We'll have to make the most of the time we have, then, won't we?"

Before they could resume their game, Cooper's and Claire's dads walked right through their court carrying what looked like a bunch of burlap sacks.

"What are you doing?" Cooper asked.

"Should we tell her, Jack?" Mr. Hughes asked in mock seriousness.

"I don't know. Do you think she's trustworthy?"

"Okay, forget I asked."

By now, Claire, Alex, Josh, and Greg were gathered around the men, too, and it was harder to ignore five quizzical teenagers.

"We thought it would be fun to have a clambake," Mr. Ellis finally said. "So there, you dragged it out of me."

"That's great!" Cooper said, oozing enthusiasm. "We've never done that before!"

"Oh, hey, Greg, didn't even see you there. Welcome back," Cooper's dad said. "Are you going to join us for the festivities? The more the merrier."

"I'll check with my parents, but it should be fine. Thanks for the invite."

"Anytime. I see you've met the rest of the gang." Mr. Ellis gestured at Alex and Josh.

"Actually, not really."

"Oh!" Cooper cried. "We were so excited to see him, Claire and I forgot to make the introductions!"

Before she could rectify her mistake, Josh and Alex did it for her, introducing themselves and shaking hands with Greg.

Cooper noticed that Josh was very quick to take her hand, as if he wanted to let Greg know she was taken or something, but she decided not to make a big deal out of it. She remembered all too well how seeing Josh and Reagan together had made her feel, and they were just friends. Of course, at that time Cooper had no assurance of how Josh felt about her, whereas now he knew exactly where he stood and was still acting insecure.

Instead of dwelling on it, though, Cooper turned her attention to watching her dad and Mr. Hughes bury their dinner in the sand. There were hot rocks involved, and then potatoes, corn, and, of course, clams were layered on top and covered with the burlap. The whole mess was then buried in a way that was supposed to ensure the food would be steamed to perfection when they dug it back up.

Cooper had her doubts, but she had to agree it was a creative way to cook. When the food was unearthed after what seemed an interminable wait, though, she was proven wrong. Everything was delicious!

"Who's up for a movie?" Greg asked once the clam shells had all been emptied of their contents and cobs were all that remained of the corn.

"Sounds like fun," Claire answered. "As long as it's okay," she added, looking to her parents for consent.

"Sure," Mrs. Hughes said. "Why don't you all go. There aren't really any dishes to do, and your vacation's almost over. You should make the most of it."

That was all the encouragement Cooper needed. "Let me just run inside and get a sweat shirt," she said, dashing off in the direction of the beach house.

Alex was always up for a movie, so there was no question involved there, but by the time Cooper returned she sensed something was amiss.

"Why aren't you going to go?" Alex was asking Josh. "There's nothing for you to do hanging around here by yourself."

"What's up?" Cooper asked, joining the conversation late.

"Josh doesn't want to go to the movie," Claire explained.

"Why not?" Cooper asked, although she thought she already knew the reason. She guessed he was telling himself that sharing her with Alex and Claire was bad enough, but he didn't want to share her with Greg, too.

"I just don't feel like a movie," Josh insisted. "But that

doesn't mean no one should go."

That was Cooper's cue to volunteer to stay behind, and she considered it—for about a second. If she caved in and let Josh have his way, though, he would think that what he was doing was okay with Cooper, that any time he didn't want her to do something he could manipulate her this way. He had admitted a week ago on this very beach that he didn't know how he would react the next time Cooper chose her friends instead of him. It seemed like it was time to find out.

"I'm really sorry you don't want to come with us," Cooper told a surprised Josh. "Are you sure you won't change your mind? We'll really miss you."

A stubborn streak Cooper had never seen seemed to emerge right before her eyes as Josh dug in his heels and insisted he was staying behind.

"Okay, then. We'll see you when we get back if you're still up."

❊   ❊   ❊

Josh wasn't awake when Cooper and the rest of the gang returned from the theater, and she had to admit she was glad. She wasn't up for another serious talk, especially if it wasn't going to get them anywhere but right back where they were now.

"Are you and Josh going to break up?" Claire asked Cooper after the girls were in bed.

"I don't know," Cooper answered honestly.

"I'd hate for you to since you seem so perfect for each other, but if he doesn't make you happy, I think you should," Claire counseled.

"What if he makes me happy sometimes and miserable others?"

"I have no idea."

"Neither do I. I've been trying to be so responsible and stick it out. I don't want to just bail as soon as things get a little difficult, you know? That seems like such an immature thing to do."

"But maybe realizing you shouldn't be in a relationship and getting out of it can be mature, too," Claire suggested.

"I've never thought of it that way," Cooper said.

"Maybe you should."

❈　　❈　　❈

"Happy birthday," Claire said as soon as Cooper opened her eyes in the morning. "How does it feel to be sixteen? You have to tell me so I'll be prepared when it's my turn."

"Sadly, it feels just like fifteen," Cooper reported. "Maybe that will change as the day goes on."

"Could be," Claire shrugged.

The wonderful aromas coming from the kitchen were enough to drag Cooper out of bed even though she could have easily slept another hour or two.

"Good morning, birthday girl," Mrs. Ellis said as soon as Cooper had descended the stairs.

Without even looking, Cooper could tell her mother was fixing pancakes and bacon and fresh-squeezed orange juice, all of her favorites.

"You're the best mom in the whole wide world," Cooper said, taking a deep breath and savoring the smells in the kitchen. "And you'll be the best mom in the whole universe once you make my cake."

"I've been meaning to talk to you about that. I have to run into the city today for a few hours, and I'm afraid if I get hung up I won't have time when I get back to make Grandma's chocolate angel food. Would you be terribly disappointed if I made it for you one night next week instead?"

"Yes, but I guess I'll get over it even though it's the only thing I asked for for my birthday," Cooper finished, sighing dramatically. She knew she was laying it on really thick. She felt sort of bad because she knew if her mom could help it, she would, but she was already getting a room makeover she didn't want. And there was still that little issue of her mother being the one who invited Josh out for the week in the first place—and now he was threatening to ruin her special day with his bad attitude.

"I'll try my best is all I can tell you," her mother replied.

Some sixteenth birthday, Cooper thought, resting her chin in her hand on the kitchen counter and pouting.

"I'll make you a cake," Claire offered.

"Thanks," Cooper mumbled. She appreciated the gesture, but it wouldn't be the same.

"You're not too old for picture pancakes, are you?" Mrs. Ellis asked.

"No," Cooper replied, half of her smile returning. "No snakes, though."

"I'll stick to bears and hearts and letters. How's that?"

"Great!"

Cooper was eating her name written in little tiny pancakes when the boys finally made an appearance.

"Are you hungry for some pancakes?" Mrs. Ellis asked.

"You bet. Bring 'em on!" Alex answered with enthusiasm.

Josh's "I'd like some, thanks," was a bit more subdued, and he didn't meet Cooper's eyes. That answered her unspoken question regarding whether he was still mad about the night before.

"It's Cooper's birthday," Claire announced halfway through the meal when it was obvious Alex and Josh weren't going to remember on their own.

"Oh, I can't believe I forgot!" Alex said. "Happy birthday!"

"Happy birthday," Josh added more quietly. He actually looked at Cooper, though, which was a big improvement, and something in his eyes seemed to say he was softening.

"You kids run along and have fun," Mrs. Ellis said when the food was done. "Your dad's out running an errand, and then we're leaving for the city as soon as he gets back. Claire's parents are coming, too, but you have a good day, sweetheart. We'll be back later, and then we can all go out for a nice dinner tonight to celebrate."

"Sounds good. And, Mom . . . thanks for the pancakes."

"Thanks for letting me make them. I don't know what I'll do when you're too old for them. I think it would break my heart to make just plain old round ones for you."

"I don't think you have to worry. There are some things I'll never outgrow," Cooper promised.

❄   ❄   ❄

Alex and Josh were in the water seeing who could swim the farthest or hold their breath the longest or something equally manly, which the girls wanted no part of.

"Let's just close our eyes and pretend we're in Tahiti, okay?" Cooper suggested.

Claire was lying on a beach towel next to her best friend, sifting the fine sand through her fingers. "You don't have to convince me. Paradise, here we come."

"Okay, there's a warm island breeze, and you can hear the palm trees gently swaying," Cooper began. "We're being served fruit juice in those funny coconut halves with umbrellas in them."

"Tell me more."

"Far away there's a Calypso band playing. . . ."

"Does Tahiti have Calypso bands?" Claire asked, sitting up and eyeing Cooper skeptically.

"In my daydreams they do. Now, lie back down or I'm going to leave you right here and return to Tahiti without you."

"I'm trying," Claire said, "but look what I just found in the sand. It's a subway token!"

Cooper took the two-tone coin and inspected it. Indeed, it was a New York City subway token. "So much for Tahiti," she said sadly.

❄   ❄   ❄

When the girls went inside for their afternoon shower, the phone rang, catching them both off guard.

"Do you think we should answer it?" Claire asked. "What if it's for the McCormicks?"

"What if it isn't?" Cooper countered.

"But who knows we're here and have this number?"

"I guess we'll find out," Cooper said, picking up the phone and saying hello.

"Hi, honey. It's Mom."

"Where are you?"

"On the Long Island Expressway. We've had some car

trouble, or I guess I should say van trouble, and we're waiting for the tow truck."

"Oh no! Are you all right?"

"Yes. There's nothing for you to worry about. We just had some engine trouble. The traffic on the L.I.E. was a little more than it could take. But the reason I'm calling is to tell you I don't know when we're going to be back. It could be hours, which means we'll miss your birthday dinner."

"Oh" was all Cooper could think to say.

"I'm so sorry. I feel just terrible."

"That's okay."

"No, it isn't, but why don't you kids go out anyway? You could call a cab and go to that cute little inn downtown. There's money on the dresser in our room."

"That's okay," Cooper said.

"Now, don't just sit around and mope. You only turn sixteen once."

It's a good thing, Cooper thought. *I don't know if I could go through this again.*

COOPER WAS SITTING in an Adirondack chair, trying to salvage what was left of the day, soaking up the last few rays, and wondering if she would ever *feel* sixteen, when Josh joined her. She hadn't seen him since her mother called, so he didn't know yet that their dinner plans were canceled. She wondered if it would matter even if she did tell him.

"Where's Greg?" he asked, jumping right into a touchy subject, and Cooper braced herself for the confrontation she had successfully avoided the night before.

"His parents made dinner reservations at some place in Southampton. Somewhere fancy, I think. He was complaining that he had to dress up on his vacation."

"Too bad," Josh replied, sounding like it was anything but.

"What's that supposed to mean?" Cooper asked, trying not to get angry.

"Nothing. I'm just not horribly disappointed that he won't be hanging around tonight is all."

"Why would he want to after the way you've been treating him?"

"Alex is just as bad. Why aren't you mad at him?"

"Because *he's* not my boyfriend," Cooper pointed out.

"I'm beginning to wonder if I am anymore, either."

Before Cooper could respond to Josh's troubling comment, Claire and Alex appeared from the kitchen with their creation: a chocolate cupcake with one candle in the middle.

"Happy birthday to you . . ." they began.

Cooper tried to paste a smile on her face, but every time she did, she would feel the corners start to droop. It was a silly song, but she didn't want her friends to think she didn't appreciate their effort.

"Make a wish," Claire directed, holding the candle just a little too close to Cooper's nose.

With her eyes closed tight, Cooper sent a silent request up to heaven and then blew out the lonely little candle. She was going to need more than a simple birthday wish to make her dreams come true.

❄   ❄   ❄

"Josh, we need to talk," Cooper said after Alex and Claire had returned to the kitchen. "You want to take a walk down the beach?"

"Sure," Josh agreed, being more amiable than he had at any point during the previous twenty-four hours.

Cooper had imagined many different scenarios over the years when she dreamed of her sixteenth birthday, and while in a few of them she may have been walking down the beach with a cute guy, in none of them was she breaking up with him. Still, she knew things weren't working out, and she had to do something whether it was her birthday or not. She took a deep breath and plunged right in.

"You know, Josh, there is never going to not be anyone else in my life. Even if I stopped hanging out with Alex and

Claire tomorrow, there would be other friends, other guys. As much as I care about you, I don't want to have just you in my world. And I don't think you should want just me, as flattering as that is. It's too much pressure. I can't be your whole life, and I've been killing myself trying to be."

"I don't want to be the only thing in your world, I just want to know I'm special."

"You are, but you can't make me keep proving that over and over. It's exhausting."

"I'm sorry," Josh finally apologized. "I guess I just kept thinking if I got you to say it enough, it would make it more true."

"It is true, but I think it's also true that I'm not ready for this relationship right now—at least, not if it stays this intense."

"What if I said I'd try to change?" Josh asked.

"I don't think it would help. You want more of me than I have to give, and I feel like I'm disappearing. Maybe I'm not ready for a relationship with anyone right now," Cooper shrugged.

"When you are, I hope I'll still be here," Josh said a little angrily.

"I hope so, too. But I know I can't ask you to wait around," Cooper admitted.

"I don't know if you even want this now," Josh said, pulling a tiny envelope out of his pocket. "Sorry I didn't have time to wrap it," he said, handing it to her.

Cooper opened it and peeked inside. It was a necklace. She poured it out into the palm of her hand and saw it was a silver cross.

"It's English," Josh offered. "I was looking for an English cross because of the reading group, and C. S. Lewis is English, and I never would have become a Christian if it weren't for you and that group."

The words came tumbling out in a jumble, but the sentiment was clear and Cooper treasured it up in her heart, even though the moment was bittersweet.

"Thank you," she said quietly as she fastened the dainty silver chain around her neck.

"No big deal," Josh shrugged, attempting to be nonchalant.

They walked back toward the beach house in silence, and Cooper wondered for the millionth time why things couldn't be different. When Josh wasn't pushing her, demanding more than she could give, they got along so great.

As if he were reading her thoughts, Josh said, "You know, this isn't how I wanted this week to go."

"I know." Cooper felt like she should say more but she couldn't think of anything, so she remained silent, raising her hand up to touch her new cross.

❉   ❉   ❉

"Where have you guys been?" Alex asked as soon as the ex-couple entered the house. "I prepared this beautiful dinner, and now it's all ruined."

"He microwaved hot dogs," Claire clarified.

"Still, I cooked!"

"Yes, you did do that."

"I'm sorry if we ruined your plans," Cooper apologized. "Did you save us anything?"

"Sure!" Alex said, jumping up. "Let me just whip something up for you. I'm a whiz in the kitchen, you know."

"No, I didn't know that," Cooper said, trying to keep a straight face.

"Just wait, and I'll prove it to you."

The hot dogs were pretty good, and Cooper treated herself to another of Claire's gourmet cupcakes when she was done. Then Alex disappeared into the bedroom he was sharing with Josh and returned with a gift bag.

"Here. Open it. Hurry!"

"Okay, okay." She felt a little self-conscious unwrapping Alex's gift while still sitting at the kitchen table with Josh, especially after everything that had happened. There was no way to gracefully decline, though, so she reached inside, grabbed the contents, and pulled it out.

"It's a picture frame," Cooper guessed before she even peeled back the tissue paper.

"No fair!" Alex cried in typical Alex fashion.

"Oh," she said, after turning it over. It was a framed miniature of the movie poster from *Beach Blanket Bingo*. She breathed a sigh of relief that it wasn't something more romantic.

"I thought this way you could remember our week at the beach," Alex explained.

"That's a great idea. I love it," Cooper told him. "I'll hang it up in my room as soon as I get home." After she made that promise, though, she wondered how long it would stay hung with her mother redoing her room soon.

After only an hour of TV, Cooper found herself yawning uncontrollably, so she said her good-nights and went to bed. She was just pulling the covers up under her chin when her parents came in.

"How was your birthday?"

"Fine," Cooper said rather than search for an adjective

that would better encompass all that had happened since that morning. There most likely wasn't one.

"Well, again, we're sorry we missed most of it. At least we have a van to drive us home in the morning, though."

"That's good," Cooper said. "But I'm sorry you had to spend your day on the expressway."

"At least you can guarantee we'll never forget your sixteenth birthday," Mr. Ellis quipped.

❄   ❄   ❄

"Cooper, are you asleep?" Claire whispered into the darkness.

"Yes."

"Forget it, then. I was just going to give you your birthday present, but never mind."

"I'm awake," Cooper said, popping upright in bed.

"I thought that might do the trick. I was trying to find the right time all day to give you this, but I never did. I'm glad I waited, though, because I was able to add a little memento of the day."

"What if I'm not sure I want to remember today?" Cooper joked.

"Why, did something happen? I mean besides you having no birthday dinner or cake or parents?"

"Josh and I broke up."

"Oh, Cooper! I'm so sorry!"

"It's okay, really. It just makes me sad, though, even though I know it was the right thing for right now."

"Open your present, and that will help cheer you up."

Cooper took the package from her friend and gently untied the ribbon. It wasn't a surprise, but Cooper still squealed with delight when she saw the Shaun Cassidy book.

"I love it! I'm going to sleep with it under my pillow," Cooper vowed, clutching the book to her chest. "Thank you."

"There's a little something else, too," Claire said, holding out a small box.

Cooper pulled off the lid, felt around under the cotton, and pulled out . . . a subway token.

"I wanted you to remember Tahiti," Claire explained. "And that maybe right where we are isn't so bad, either."

"I'll treasure it always," Cooper vowed, clutching the coin to her chest.

"My dad can drill a hole in it for you when we get home. That way you can put it on your key chain or something so it doesn't get mixed up with your other tokens and you accidentally use it."

"Good idea."

"Cooper?" Claire said timidly after the light was turned out for the third time that night.

"Yeah?"

"I know this probably isn't a good time to tell you this, but I have a date with Matt tomorrow night and I really need someone to be excited for me."

"Claire, that's great! Why didn't you tell me sooner? When did he ask you?"

"He asked me last Friday after school, but I told him we were going out of town. That's when he suggested tomorrow after I get back. I'm meeting him at Cuppa Joe."

"That still doesn't explain why you kept it a secret all week," Cooper pointed out.

"I guess I just wanted to hang on to it a little longer. I wanted to take my time getting used to the idea and not rush things. I knew as soon as I said it out loud it would change."

"I can understand that," Cooper replied. "I'm all for taking things slow, especially now."

"Thanks."

"You're welcome. Now, good night!" Cooper said sternly, but she was laughing as she did. "I don't know why no one in this house wants me to go to sleep!"

16

THE MOOD AT THE BEACH HOUSE was decidedly somber the next morning. The adults were tired from their adventure the day before, Cooper and Josh were emotionally drained, and Alex was sorry to be leaving and going back to school. The only one with a smile on her face was Claire because she had a date waiting for her back in Manhattan.

"Don't forget to check in the dresser drawers and under the beds, kids, to be sure you're not forgetting anything," Mrs. Ellis reminded.

"If you start bringing your stuff down, I'm ready to load the van," Mr. Ellis added.

It seemed to take much longer to pack up than it did to unpack, Cooper noticed. Maybe it had to do with a lack of enthusiasm, or maybe everything had just spread out during their week at the sea. Either way, it was an hour before they had the van loaded with both belongings and passengers.

"We didn't get to say good-bye to Greg," Claire said as they drove off.

"That's a real shame," Alex teased.

Cooper forced herself not to look at Josh to see his expression.

They stopped at a little white church for the Sunday

morning service before leaving the island altogether. It was a nice transition. The pastor wasn't particularly eloquent, but he had a simple message: God doesn't want you to succeed as much as He wants you to just keep trying. He went on to explain how we come to know God by seeking Him. By messing up and learning and picking ourselves up and running after God again.

"Don't worry if you don't feel like you've arrived," the pastor said in his comforting way. "That just means you're still willing to learn what God has to teach you. The process is what's important. Besides, if you're perfect, there's no room for God to teach you about grace. Remember, He doesn't give us what we deserve. He shows mercy to us and blesses us beyond what we have a right to expect."

Cooper thought about that message all the way back to Manhattan. She'd felt like such a failure lately. In her modeling career, in her relationship with Josh, in her faith. But she had certainly learned a lot about herself from the mistakes she'd made. Did that make it worth it? She wasn't sure, but it made her feel better to know it was okay to still be "in process."

Alex and Josh were dropped off along the way, which only increased Cooper's antsiness to get to her own home. When they pulled up in front of her apartment building, Cooper couldn't wait to run up to her room, throw herself across her bed, and just lie there like a lump, but she had to help unload the van first. Her dad and Mr. Hughes were taking it back right away. It took two trips to get everything upstairs without the boys to help, and when they finished, her mom insisted she stay downstairs.

"I just need to talk to your father for a minute," she explained.

"What does that have to do with me? Why can't I go upstairs?"

"Because I asked you to wait."

Cooper stayed, but she huffed and puffed and tapped her foot impatiently the whole time. Claire and her mom had already disappeared, and she didn't understand why she couldn't, too.

"So you'll be back for dinner within the hour?" Mrs. Ellis asked her husband through the van's driver-side window.

"Yes. We'll make it as fast as we can," he promised.

"Okay, we'll see you then."

"*Now* can go I upstairs?" Cooper asked.

"Yes," her mother answered, ignoring her daughter's tone.

"Why did I have to wait with you?" Cooper asked again.

"Maybe I just like having you close by," she answered, putting her arm around Cooper and giving her a hug.

"You're so weird sometimes!" Cooper replied, laughing, before hugging her mom back.

"Now, don't go messing your room all up after you got it so clean before vacation," Mrs. Ellis warned.

Cooper picked up her suitcase from where she had dumped it in the entryway. "I won't," she said. All she wanted to do was lie down on her familiar bed in her familiar room, where boyfriends and sixteenth birthdays and problems of any kind didn't exist. But when she entered her room, Cooper was confused. She looked back out in the hallway to make sure it was familiar, that they hadn't somehow ended up in the wrong apartment.

She was in the right apartment, all right, but her familiar room was no longer familiar. The walls were painted a faint silver, and on her bed was a new deep blue comforter cover with silver stars. On top of it were silver, blue, and yellow pillows in various sizes and shapes made of velvet with little patterns burned into them. Some had spirals on them and others had moons or stars. Her headboard was different, too. It was padded and covered with silver velvet with stars imprinted on it. On the window was a valance of the same fabric as the comforter cover, and hanging under it was a sheer silvery curtain covered with pockets. Upon closer inspection Cooper saw that each pocket was filled with a photo. She and Claire when they were babies. Alex and the girls back in junior high. Her parents. Aunt Penny. She and Josh before the dance. One of the test shots she did for Yakomina. A few of the pockets had silver stars in them instead of pictures.

Most amazing of all, her flannelgraph characters had made the cut. Above her desk was a bulletin board covered in midnight blue felt, with silver stars dancing across the top and the women of the Old Testament displayed across the bottom. Other things were the same, too. Knickknacks, pictures, and other collectibles were still out in the open, but they had just been grouped a little better. Her favorite collection of shells was even in a display box that now hung on the wall.

"Well, what do you think?" her mom asked, peering cautiously into the new room.

"It's amazing!" Cooper said and meant it.

"Are you sure you like it? I know we have pretty different tastes, but I tried to take that into consideration and remember it's your room."

"It's amazing!" Cooper repeated, shaking her head in wonder. She had been so against this idea. So certain her mother didn't know her well enough to create a room Cooper would want to live in.

"This is why we were all in Manhattan yesterday."

"I wondered what work you had that couldn't wait," Cooper said.

"I had to make sure the painting went okay, and then we were using the van to bring in your new headboard."

"I had no idea."

"So you were really surprised?" Mrs. Ellis asked, seeming pleased with herself.

"Definitely."

"And you really like it?"

"Absolutely," Cooper nodded.

"Good, I'm so relieved."

"So am I," Cooper admitted, then clapped her hand over her mouth.

"Sooo, you didn't think I could pull it off, eh?" Mrs. Ellis grinned.

"No, that's not it at all," Cooper tried to explain.

"It's okay, sweetheart. I know what you meant. Remember I had a mother once, too, you know."

"So I hear," Cooper joked. Then, turning serious, she gave her mom a huge bear hug. "Thanks."

"For the room?"

"For everything. For giving me more than I deserve."

"It was my pleasure. Now, why don't you come help me with the chocolate angel food."

I DOUBT I'D BE ABLE TO WRITE a single intelligible sentence if it weren't for the support and encouragement of the OHs. You're all a part of me. And to the CCMers who've made Nashville not just fun but home. Rock on.

Young Adult Fiction Series From Bethany House Publishers
(Ages 12 and up)

— ∞∞∞ —

CEDAR RIVER DAYDREAMS • by Judy Baer
Experience the challenges and excitement of high
school life with Lexi Leighton and her friends.

GOLDEN FILLY SERIES • by Lauraine Snelling
Tricia Evanston races to become the first female jockey
to win the sought-after Triple Crown.

JENNIE MCGRADY MYSTERIES • by Patricia Rushford
A contemporary Nancy Drew, Jennie McGrady's
sleuthing talents bring back readers again and again.

LIVE! FROM BRENTWOOD HIGH • by Judy Baer
The staff of an action-packed teen-run news show ex-
plores the love, laughter, and tears of high school life.

PASSPORT TO DANGER • by Mary Reeves Bell
Constantine Rea, an American living in modern-day
Austria, confronts the lasting horrors of the Holocaust.

THE SPECTRUM CHRONICLES • by Thomas Locke
Adventure awaits readers in this fantasy series set in
another place and time.

SPRINGSONG BOOKS • by various authors
Compelling love stories and contemporary themes
promise to capture the hearts of readers.

UNMISTAKABLY COOPER ELLIS • by Wendy Lee Nentwig
Laugh and cry with Cooper as she strives to balance
modeling, faith, and life at her Manhattan high school.

WHITE DOVE ROMANCES • by Yvonne Lehman
Romance, suspense, and fast-paced action for teens
committed to finding pure love.